Ghost in the Turret

Ghost in the Turret

Donna Wren Carson

BOOKSIDE Press

Copyright © 2024 by Donna Wren Carson

ISBN: 978-1-77883-467-7 (Paperback)

All rights reserved. No part of this publication may be reproduced, distributed, or transmitted in any form or by any means, including photocopying, recording, or other electronic or mechanical methods, without the prior written permission of the publisher, except in the case brief quotations embodied in critical reviews and other noncommercial uses permitted by copyright law.

The views expressed in this book are solely those of the author and do not necessarily reflect the views of the publisher, and the publisher hereby disclaims any responsibility for them.

BookSide Press
877-741-8091
www.booksidepress.com
orders@booksidepress.com

DEDICATION

I dedicate this book to my beautiful, cherished daughter Ariel and my dearest lifetime friend Laura. Both sparked my imagination with some events that gave inspiration to this piece of literature. Thank you, both.

Summary

Leira MacGregor is invited to stay at Skye Finnegan's' home during spring vacation while her parents go to Aruba. Ecstatically, their best friend Addy Davies is welcome to stay also.

Already warned that Skye's turreted guest room's attic is out of limits, they defiantly investigate and encounter strange and terrifying events. They conquer numerous fears with the help of an old friend and an unexpected ally. Then, winding their way through a series of hair-raising adventures, they come face to face with a ghost in a triangle of Mysteries.

The three best friends (LAS) are united together again to solve their most fearsome and deadly adventure yet. While Leira and Addy are staying with Skye, they investigate "The Ghost" in the attic. Emotions heighten as threatening messages appear. Are the messages truly from the grave? They seek the advice—or help, from astonishing sources, but it might be too late for one person has already died.

Contents

Summary vii

Chapter 1: Spring Vacation 1
Chapter 2: The Surrounding Wilderness 6
Chapter 3: Someone Follows 13
Chapter 4: Ghost In The Attic? 18
Chapter 5: Questions? 23
Chapter 6: Investigation 28
Chapter 7: Mysterious Intruder 34
Chapter 8: A New Accomplice 39
Chapter 9: Another Night In The Turret 45
Chapter 10: The Confrontation 50
Chapter 11: Blood in the Attic 56
Chapter 12: More Research 61
Chapter 13: Notes And Phone Calls 67
Chapter 14: Cherry-O-Cream Pie and Mrs. Finnegan 73
Chapter 15: Sell the House? 79
Chapter 16: Murder Or Suicide? 86
Chapter 17: The Puzzle Starts To Come Together 92
Chapter 18: Ready To Face The Ghost 98
Chapter 19: Not For Sale—You Can't Threaten Us 105
Chapter 20: 5 Heads Crack The Case 113

Chapter 1

Spring Vacation

Spring vacation was only a few weeks away. My best friends, Addy Davies, Skye Finnegan, and I walked to school on this chilly, windy day. I asked them, "So, have your parents told you what you were going to do during vacation?"

Skye, with her shoulder-length, nutmeg brown hair blowing in the wind, grinned and replied gently, "My parents haven't said a word, but I know they're planning something."

Addy grimaced and replied, "I'm sure my parents know what's going on, but no matter how much I bug them, they won't tell me a thing." As she brushed back a strand of her hair from her eyes, she said, "I just hope whatever we are doing that my little sister Josie isn't included!"

Looking towards me, Addy questioned, "Leira, you're the one who's figured out your parents are going somewhere special for vacation, but you just don't know where. Do you think there's any chance that they'll take us with you again like your Mom took us to Arizona in February?"

I sighed, twirling several strands of my extra-long, honey-brown hair around my fingers, and replied a bit irritably, "You know what? I've got a bad feeling that they aren't even going to take me with them."

Skye and Addy looked utterly astonished, and then Skye exclaimed, "NO WAY!"

I replied dismally, "After our last 'adventure' in Arizona, I think my Mom is afraid to take us or me anywhere."

Addy shot back, "Why? If it's just you, then your Mom shouldn't really have anything to worry about."

Shrugging my shoulders, I responded, "I don't know. It's just a feeling I have. It's kind of like twos' company, but three is a crowd."

Addy shook her newly cropped, thick, blackish-brown hair and said crisply, "I can't believe that neither one of you have said anything about my new haircut." Shaking her head again, she gave Skye and me one of her typical gleeful smiles.

Grinning, I reminisced about the day I first met Addy. She was the most cheerful person I had ever known, although sometimes she could be the worst fraidy cat. Both she and Skye had moved into my neighborhood during the previous summer. We were now finishing our last few months at J.P. Gooding's Elementary School. In the fall, the three of us would be starting Middle school. Each of us was extremely nervous about starting seventh grade.

I replied exasperatingly to Addy's question, "You know I love your new haircut. I've already told you that at least fifty times! The only thing I want to know is why you cut it 'before' vacation. Why didn't you cut it during the holiday, so everyone will see the 'new you' afterward?"

Addy shrugged her shoulders and replied embarrassingly, "Probably because my Mom said I had to. Hey—what if it's because we are going somewhere that my Mom doesn't know where to get it cut? What about you, Leira? Are you ever going to cut your hair? It's almost past your butt now!"

Thoughtfully, I sifted my fingers through my long, shiny hair and replied, "I don't know. My grandpa told me never to cut it…but maybe someday…"

Before I could finish explaining, a gruff voice shouted out from behind us, "Hey, Addy! Wait up!"

Looking behind us, we groaned in disgust as we watched Addy's somewhat new neighbor, Jeffrey, hurrying to catch up with us. Addy and I quickened our steps because our school was close. However, Skye stopped, turned around, and with her pretty, round face now scrunched up in anger, she halted Jeffrey with blazing eyes and stated loudly, "JEFFREY KUVASC! This is the last time I'm warning you to leave Addy alone. The next time you bother her, I'm going to tell my brother

Liam." She squinted her eyes angrily at him one last time before turning around and jogging off to catch up with us.

As Skye approached, breathing hard, Addy exclaimed, "Thanks,—you're the best friend ever! Do you really think your brother would stand up for me?"

Skye hesitated before replying, "Probably not, because Liam's such a bully himself. But I think his reputation would scare anyone away—even Jeffrey!"

Addy and I tried to hide our grins after Skye's reply. But in the corner of my eye, I saw a slight smirk on her face too.

Suddenly feeling irritated, I added, "I still can't believe it's been almost two months since Jeffrey moved next door to you, Addy. Remember how happy we were when we found out he was moving. No wonder why he didn't tell anyone where he was moving to."

Skye added sarcastically, "And we thought old Mrs. Crimpton was bad." Addy looked a bit downcast as she replied, "Well, since he's moved in, he hasn't been as nasty to me. I mean, well… he's still a trouble-maker, but when I'm outside, he doesn't bother me much."

Skye replied, grinning humorously, "That's because he likes you!"

Looking at Skye in horror, Addy hit her gently with her purse, demanding, "You take that back, Skye Finnegan!"

Raising an eyebrow, I laughed and then teased Addy, " I thought you just told Skye that she was the best friend ever." Addy lowered her head, slightly discomfited, but didn't say a word. Glancing back at Jeffrey, I tried to imagine that there might be a tiny bit of good in him.

A week before spring vacation, my parents finally made their announcement. Upon arriving home from school, Mom was busy making barbecued pork chops with garlic mashed potatoes and buttery corn on the cob. The spicy aroma made my stomach grumble. Slightly confused, I asked, "Mom, why are you home so early and making dinner now?"

Just then, Dad walked around the corner as my dogs, Lucky and Fluffums, raced towards me, squealing happily. I stooped down, and they smothered my face with sloppy wet kisses. Laughing while I embraced them, I looked up at my parents and asked once again, "What's going on?"

I wasn't worried because they both looked happy. I was more curious than anything.

Mom moistened her lips before replying, "Well, we have good and bad news."

Anxiously, I asked, "And…what's the good news?"

Mom and Dad exchanged glances, and then Mom replied, "Well, the good news is that we're going to Aruba for vacation."

I was absolutely ecstatic. My parents had been there three times and told me how awesome it was and showed me all their pictures. I couldn't believe I was finally going to go. Then, sensing their discomfort, I asked tentatively, "So… what's the bad news—aren't Skye or Addy invited?"

My dad replied sympathetically, "Mom and I are going alone. You're not going with us—at least this time."

I screamed, "WHAT? What do you mean, I'm not going with you… that's not fair… you can't do that… I have to go… I've been waiting forever!" I continued shouting out all the reasons why they had to take me until Dad gave me his 'look' and raised his hand for me to stop. I shut my mouth, and with tears glistening in my eyes, looked up at them for an explanation.

Mom responded consolingly, "I know how much you want to go, but Dad and I need some time for ourselves, and it's our 20th anniversary."

Dejectedly, I glanced downwards as tears began streaming down my face. Looking up at Mom, I uttered, "I get it. You just want time without me."

Dad looked me straight in the eye and said, "Not exactly." Pausing, he then added, "We thought you, Lucky, and Fluffums would like to stay at Skye's for vacation."

While trying to understand what they were saying, someone started knocking loudly on our front door. Then I heard Addy and Skye yelling, "Leira! Let us in! We have something important to tell you."

Completely confused, I glanced from the door to my parents. Smiling, my mother asked, "What are you waiting for? Go answer the door."

With my head spinning, I raced to the door, and after swinging it open, I saw Skye and Addy standing on my front porch with enormous smiles on both their faces. Shaking my head in confusion, I asked, "What the HECK is going on? My parents are going to ARUBA without me!"

Skye looked at me, grinning slyly, and questioned, "Yeah… but, where are YOU staying?"

Addy nodded her head enthusiastically and added, "NO! Where are WE staying?"

As the answer dawned on me, I didn't let either of them know how excited I was. Instead, I pursed my lips and said dejectedly, "Not in Aruba."

Skye punched my arm lightly as Addy stated, "No! Both you and I are going to stay at Skye's house."

"AND, we're going to get to sleep in the turreted guest room! Isn't that awesome?" she questioned.

Sheepishly, I looked at them and asked Addy suspiciously, "No Josie?"

Addy smiled happily and replied, "Nope! My parents have told my annoying little sister to stay away—REALLY!"

Looking at Skye, I asked, "What about your brother Liam?"

Smugly, Skye replied, "He's going to camp for a few days, and then he's spending the rest of the week with a new friend. So, it's just the three of us in the turret room, with on-demand TV, a fridge full of soda, and a cabinet full of snacks—not to mention every DVD that we love!"

My parents were standing just out of sight. But after Skye's statement, Mom came into the living room and asked, "Leira, I hope you understand that you're going to take care of your pets. That means all of them, Fluffums, Lucky, and your cat Emmy while we're gone. Is that clear?"

"Absolutely!" I replied proudly, then added, "But next time, I get to go to Aruba—WITH Skye AND Addy!"

Mom grinned and said, "We'll see about that."

Chapter 2

The Surrounding Wilderness

Strangely, I was excited and feeling sad the final week before vacation. Part of me was angry and feeling left out that my parents were going to Aruba without me. But, on the positive side, Addy and I were going to spend a week with Skye in her parent's specially built turreted guest bedroom. The last time we had slept there was for Skye's twelfth birthday. Most of the kids invited were anxious because Mrs. Finnegan had told everyone not to go into the turret's attic. She said it wasn't safe. But Addy, Skye, and I thought by the uneasy way Mrs. Finnegan had replied that something more mysterious or sinister was behind her warning.

After Skye and Addy happily left my house, I continued to complain about not going to Aruba. But eventually, I realized that I would probably have a better time at Skye's. Before I gave in completely to my parent's announcement, I pleaded one last time with them to let Skye, Addy, and myself go to Aruba. Mom sternly replied, "Let's just see how this vacation goes. If everything goes well, then maybe we can take another trip with your friends."

The following week, my parents headed to the airport to catch a flight to Aruba. Watching them leave, I felt miserable. Skye, sensing my disappointment, put her arm around my shoulder and gave me a brief hug. Addy listened as Skye asked inquisitively, "What about that old fort you told us about?"

Addy hastened to add, "Yeah—what about the 'Rusty Creek' and the 'desert with cow bones'? You can show us everything while your parents are gone."

My eyes began to sparkle, remembering my adventures over the past few years. Then I replied, "No one can do any of that until—you climb the big tree!"

Apprehensively, Addy asked, "What do you mean? I've never climbed trees—at least—not big ones."

Skye laughed, replying, "I think that's about to change—if you want to go with us."

As Addy shuffled her feet and searched for something to say, my thoughts drifted off to what my parents had said. They had left me in the care of the Finnegan's, and even though Addy was staying with us, we had to check in with her parents a few times a day. Addy's troublesome little sister, Josie, was staying with a close neighbor. But Addy had certain times to check in on her. Josie was a bright but jealous child who always wanted to do what Addy was doing—or if not—she was looking for ways to get her older sister in trouble. Josie had already been a problem several times in the past. I hoped that during this vacation, it wouldn't happen again.

Skye interrupted my thoughts, asking, "Which tree? Which one is the 'BIG' tree?"

Happily, I responded with a secretive grin, "Follow me." We trudged through dense brush and skirted large, barren, dead branches behind my house. The tree wasn't far behind my house. It stood shortly beyond our property line, where the land sloped downward, then ditched steeply to a small meandering stream. After a few minutes of carefully maneuvering down the incline, I stopped just short of the sharp decline down to the creek. On the edge of the drop-off was rooted an enormous hemlock tree. I raised both my arms skyward and pronounced, "Here it is!"

Skye and Addy, who had been watching their footing while following me, steadied themselves and slowly lifted their gaze upwards at the 'TREE.' Addy inhaled intensely and gasped, "I know what tree this is. I can see the top half of it from my dining room window. You've got to be kidding. It's the tallest one in the woods!"

Skye, who was frightened of truly little, surveyed the deep ravine that ended with the stream. Then she said gravely, "Leira, that tree—is only back a foot or two from the drop off to the creek below. I can even see the roots coming out on the steep side. And I don't see any way to start climbing it from the safe side. The good limbs are too high to reach."

I replied confidently, "I know it seems that way, but here's the trick; do you see that short, sturdy branch about five feet up on the right?"

Addy asked skeptically, "Do you mean that stub right near the edge of the cliff?"

Skye added disdainfully, "It's not a cliff Addy. It's just a short drop off."

"Yeah—a twenty-foot drop-off!" she exclaimed.

Skye smirked and replied, "It's not even half that."

Without acknowledging Addy's scathing look, Skye turned to me and then asked, "And HOW do we climb this tree?"

I replied matter-of-factly. "You run, jump, and grab onto that branch."

Upon seeing the expressions on my friend's faces, I continued, "Don't worry, I'll show you how easy it is."

I backed up a few feet, then ran toward the tree and jumped up, grabbing hold of the short, thick branch. Glancing back at them, I called out, "Once you have a good grip, you just swing your feet up and catch that branch above." Demonstrating, I swung up, grasping the upper branch with my leg, and said, "See—it's no problem." Afterward, I released my leg, gave a little swing backward, and was standing near my friends.

Interrupting, Addy questioned in terror, "You want ME to run—jump—grab hold of that small branch and swing my feet up, wrapping them around the one just above it? What do you think I am? A MONKEY??"

Skye laughed uncontrollably, but I tried to remain upbeat and stated, "Addy, it's not as dangerous as you think. You've done a lot of more frightening things in the past. The three of us solved the 'Mystery of Grimly Manor,' and our experience in Arizona was A LOT more than an adventure."

Addy looked embarrassed and heartened at the same time. She knew she had overcome numerous fears over our times together, so she stiffened up and said, "Alright. If I make it that far—what happens next?"

Skye nodded her approval at Addy's question and then waited for my response.

I replied with a cheerful smile, "After that, it's smooth climbing. By the way, I brought my camera along so that we can take pictures from the top."

As Addy's eyes opened wider and Skye muttered, "The top?"

Reminding them, I stated, "I'm not taking you across the 'Rusty Creek' and through 'The Desert' if you don't climb the 'Big Tree'! Plus—did I mention the old, haunted school bus nearby?"

Both Addy and Skye didn't seem to know whether that was supposed to encourage them or not. I continued, "I'll show you the first couple of steps again, and then one of you can go. I'll follow, then pass you, and guide you both up to the top. It's only the first few steps that seem scary—really!"

I ran up, jumped, and held on to the stubby branch; swinging twice, I wrapped my right leg around the longer, thicker, limb above it. Then, after steadying myself, I turned my leg and raised myself into a kneeling position, allowing myself to reach up and grab hold of the next higher branch. After that, I stood up, grabbing hold of a sturdy branch about three feet above me. Confidently, I looked down at Skye and Addy and said, "See? It's not hard."

Addy exclaimed, "Yeah... if you're a gymnast!"

I climbed down quickly and, facing them, said, "I'll show you again, but then you need to decide whether you want to do it or not. Encouragingly, I said to Skye and Addy, "Remember—after those three steps, it's easy climbing to the top!"

It didn't surprise me that Skye responded first, "OK. I'll try it. But first I want to see you do it again and what the next two steps are, because if you're going to climb around me after that, then I want to see it."

Happily, I replied, "That's a great idea—watch." I swung up, wrapped my leg around the next branch, reached and pulled myself up, then climbed two easy steps upwards.

Glancing down, I asked Skye, "Are you ready?"

Skye replied, "Yeah. Come back down and talk me through this." Addy looked on worriedly.

I knew Skye was not as athletic as I was, but she had more determination and less fear than most people I knew. Apprehensively, I watched as she ran, jumped, and caught hold of the first branch. Even before I could offer her encouragement, she swung not twice but once to wrap her leg around the second branch!

Watching from below in amazement, I called up to her, "Turn your knee so you can grab the next branch."

In astonishment, I heard Skye retort, "I KNOW what to do—just shut up."

Quietly, but nervously, I waited. After a moment or two, Skye turned her leg and quickly reached up to the next branch and pulled herself upright.

Perspiring a little, she glanced down at Addy and me and then stated loudly, "All right, Leira. Get up here, and we'll talk Addy through this." After maneuvering my way up and around Skye, she looked down at Addy and said smugly, "Your turn."

Addy blanched and waited several seconds before replying bravely, "No problem."

She ran, jumped, and tried to grab the stumpy branch, but her fingers only grazed it. Looking slightly embarrassed, she yelled up to us, "That was only a practice run." Once again, she ran, leaped, and grabbed hold of the branch, only to have her fingers slide off, tearing some skin from them.

Skye and I felt terrible, but I knew Addy could do it. I yelled down, "That was almost perfect, Addy. This time, when you reach up, imagine that Jeffrey is behind you and will catch you if you don't get up!"

Addy ran, jumped, and in one fluid motion with sheer determination, grabbed the stub, wrapped her leg around the upper branch, and lifted herself into a kneeling position. From that moment, it took her less than five seconds to come level with Skye.

Addy's face blazed with happiness as Skye and I looked at her in awe.

There was no need for words of congratulations, so I began the long climb up and around the hundred-foot high hemlock tree, talking my friends through each footstep. Within a half-hour, we reached the top, where we perched slightly precariously on three different small but sturdy branches. The actual highest point of the tree was about another seven or eight feet above us.

My friends were awestruck as they gazed around at the neighborhood below. Grimly Manor, with its surrounding graveyard, looked particularly impressive. The aroma coming from the hemlock tree itself was very soothing. We stayed at the top for over an hour until I realized the sun was sinking quickly toward the horizon.

At that point, I said, "We'd better start climbing down now." I tried to keep the urgency from my voice. I said, "Skye, let me climb down between you and Addy. That's the best way for me to point out the next steps."

Addy and Skye voiced their agreement, not perceiving that I was concerned over the lateness of the hour. Slowly we began our descent. We were more than halfway down when Skye gave me a suspicious look and asked, "Is everything OK?"

I had just talked Addy down to the next branch. Glancing up at Skye, I replied quietly, "Why don't you get below me? The sun is going down, and even though I can get down in the dark, I don't think either of you should try it." Knowing Skye was brave, with a capital 'B,' she nodded her head, climbed down over me, and moved quickly to the branch above Addy.

As Addy saw Skye above her, she asked anxiously, "Where's Leira?" Skye replied casually, "She wants to get the best picture of the sunset. Keep going."

Skye was like a sergeant in the Army as she hurried Addy down to the ground. I took my time because I did want to get some beautiful pictures, but when I was about fifteen feet from the bottom, I saw something next to me move!

Skye and Addy were on the ground waiting for me when I froze in my steps! There was a squirrel less than two feet from me. Stunned, I moved my head as little as possible, gazing around to see if there were any more. There were—but a few branches higher. Down below, Addy and Skye were calling to me to hurry up, and with all my heart, I wanted to scream, "SHUT UP!"

Cautiously, with my heart hammering, I slowly crept down to the next branch. Seeing that my rodent 'friends' weren't following, I descended the rest of the tree faster than I ever had in my life.

After swinging down from the bottom branch and coming to rest at Skye's feet, I tried to calm my breathing as Addy demanded, "What took you so long? It's almost dark."

I gathered my thoughts before saying, "I saw a squirrel, and I wanted to get some good sunset pictures."

We hurried to Skye's house for our first night of vacation. I thought the most frightening part of our vacation had already happened. Little did I know squirrels were the least of my fears?

Chapter 3

Someone Follows

Dusk turned into nighttime while Addy, Skye, and I laid cozily in one of the beds of her parent's extraordinary guestroom, topped with a Victorian Turret. It was so cool. The room contained not only two sets of four-posted curtained bunk beds but also had an over-sized plasma TV, a refrigerator, and a snack-food bar. A small bathroom now stood in the little alcove that used to be a closet.

"Wow!" I exclaimed. "This seems even more awesome than when we slept over for your birthday last November."

Skye shrugged her shoulders and replied, "Well, my parents added the bathroom, and I think because there's only three of us, it probably seems bigger."

Addy gazed around happily and said, "Without everyone else, it's like a luxury suite in a fancy hotel." Jokingly, she inquired, "Do your parents have room service?"

Skye replied smugly, "Of course." She immediately picked up the phone and pressed a button. Apparently, her Mom answered quickly because Skye stated swiftly, "We'd like one large extra cheese pizza, please, and deliver it to the 'Turret Room.'"

Laughing uncontrollably as Skye hung up the phone, I gasped out, "I can't believe you said that!"

Skye grinned and said haughtily, "My Mom already knew what was coming."

After watching spooky movies and stuffing ourselves full of pizza, we each settled into our cozy beds. Annoyingly, I couldn't help but remember that the last time I was here was for Skye's birthday almost six months ago. Her mother had warned us not to go into the attic because it wasn't safe. Unfortunately, I had chosen the upper bunk bed directly beneath the square opening to the turret attic.

I didn't fall asleep quickly. My mind strayed between reality and sleep, and my imagination disturbed me, wondering what was wrong in the attic above me.

Halfway through the night, I awoke abruptly to the rumble of thunder. The next thing I saw was a flash of lightning, then a louder thunderclap, and afterward, the sound of torrential rain. I lay awake, watching and listening until the storm began to subside. It was later before sleep captured me once more that I heard creaking above me. Suddenly alert, I listened more intently—and after ten minutes or so, I detected another creak! Ready to wake my friends, but feeling like I might be over-reacting, I decided to wait another few moments. As time trickled by, my eyes kept getting heavier, and before I heard anything else, I fell deeply asleep.

Addy pounced on me in the early morning. Enthusiastically, she shook me and said, "Wake up, sleepyhead—we have to go take care of Lucky, Fluffums, and Emmy. Also, I'm starving, so I can't wait much longer for our breakfast."

Groggily, I asked, "What time is it?"

Addy replied, "Almost eight o'clock."

Groaning, I asked, "Is Skye awake?"

Skye replied grumpily, "Yeah. Addy woke me up a few minutes ago. But she's right; we have to go take care of your pets. I'm beginning to wish your parents had taken you with them."

Spitefully, I threw my pillow at Skye and hit her straight in the face. Skye flinched and said, "Sorry, I really didn't mean that the way it sounded. Let's go take care of everything and come back for breakfast… then maybe we can go on that adventure of yours."

Addy reacted, perplexed, "What Adventure?"

Annoyed, Skye replied while yawning, "Leira told us yesterday that if we climbed the big tree, she would take us into the woods. Remember—through the 'desert,' past the cow bones and haunted bus—to the secret tree house?"

Addy's eyes widened considerably as she recalled the conversation, then turning to me, she beamed and replied, "Skye's right! You're taking us there today—RIGHT?"

"Well, I replied, "If your parents let you go exploring for about three hours, then we'll go."

Addy asked apprehensively, "And what do I tell my parents?"

Skye replied quickly, "We'll tell our parents we have a science project to do during vacation, and Leira knows these woods because she's lived here most of her life."

Addy glanced at me and said, "Well, actually—I do have a science project to do, but it's not due for another month. "Leira, can we bring back plants or something that we don't have in our yards?"

I replied confidently, "Yeah. There are thistle bushes, skunk cabbage, and cattails. And—if you want—we can even bring home some tadpoles!"

"Huh?" Skye asked, slightly confused.

Addy looked at her a bit condescendingly and replied, "Tadpoles are baby frogs."

Skye laughed and replied, "I know that. I thought you said tad bolts, which I think my dad uses in his workroom."

After a slightly uncomfortable silence, I asked Skye, "Do you think your parents will let you go hiking in the woods?"

Skye answered immediately, "As long as I tell them we're going hiking with you and that you've been there before. I'm sure it'll be fine—especially if you have your cellphone Leira."

"Right then!" I replied cheerfully in my best Scottish brogue. "Let's get everything done and get going!"

After having crispy cereal, orange juice, and toast with homemade grape jam for breakfast (yum-yum), we headed to my house to take care of my two dogs and sweet cat Emmy. Addy and Skye had already gotten permission to go on a hike before their parents left for work. Mrs. Davies (now a second-grade teacher) stayed home during spring vacation, so we didn't need to worry about Addy's little sister Josie bothering us.

We traipsed through the dampened ground, down through my backyard to the old, BIG, hemlock tree. The three of us stood there, then Addy nervously inquired, "Are we going to have to climb that again?"

Trying to keep a straight face, I asked Addy in a grave tone, "Is that a problem?" Before she could answer, I laughed and replied, "NO—we don't have to climb the tree—but there'll be other things to do!"

Addy seemed relieved but slightly nervous too.

I clambered down a steep incline slightly to the left of the 'BIG' tree, which was easy enough. When I reached the edge of the brook, I looked back and noticed my friends were more carefully tracing my path. When they caught up, Skye asked, "Well—what's next?"

I replied casually, "We cross the brook."

Addy asked irritably, "And how do we do that? It's at least four feet across and more than a foot deep. If I get my shoes and pants ruined, my Mom will ground me for a week!"

I looked at Addy and replied, "Don't worry—both of you have great balance and see those logs—they'll get us across without a drop. While exploring during the last few years, I rolled those three logs together so I could get across without wading through anymore. Watch me." The logs were fastened loosely together, and I made it to the opposite side of the brook without incident. When I reached the other bank, I turned and asked, "Well?"

Skye said, "No problem—here I come." Skye traversed the 'bridge' quickly.

Addy, encouraged by Skye's easy crossing, followed her. (Little did we know that we had an unwanted and dangerous companion)?

As we continued on, I mentioned to my friends that my grandfather had promised me that he would build me a nice sturdy bridge the next time he visited. I told Skye and Addy that he was a carpenter by trade and ran a hardware store, which he sold when he retired.

I led my friends down through the deep, thick brush, past an old, crumbled dirt cave, through the spiked bushes, and finally to the 'Rusty Creek.'

Skye gasped, "Whoa! No wonder why you call it the 'Rusty Creek'"

I explained, "It's just from the minerals here, but it is really cool. The hard part is over now. This creek is small, so we just follow it a bit further, then jump across—into the desert…"

Meanwhile, Addy's little sister Josie had lied to her mother and was secretly following us. She crossed the brook with ease but was having a difficult time keeping quiet behind us.

Addy, Skye, and I followed the stream a little way and then jumped over at the narrowest part. The stream was slightly swollen from the rain the previous night, but we made the leap perfectly.

After successfully crossing the 'Rusty Creek,' I looked back at my friends—smiled—and asked secretly, "Are you ready for the desert?"

Both of them grinned, nodded, and proceeded to follow me. (Josie was a short way behind)

We started across 'the desert,' but I quickly noticed that the sand sunk in much more than I had ever experienced because of the heavy rain the previous night. I stopped my friends and said, "This ground is really, really wet, so I think you should stay behind me while I check the steps."

Addy murmured nervously, "Okay…"

I tested each footstep I took and then encouraged my friends to do the same. We were about halfway across 'the desert' when I pointed out to them the bleached cow bones lying barely within sight.

Addy scrunched up her face in disgust as Skye kept her eyes fixated on my steps—then grumbled, "Let's keep going."

Both followed me for another ten minutes or so when I finally stopped and exclaimed, "This is the end of the desert! Just up ahead is the forest where our treehouse is—not to mention the pond, where you can get your tadpoles, Addy."

Just as I was about to comment on the old 'haunted' school bus—a piercing scream rang out… and continued. It did not take Addy long to recognize the voice—it was Josie, and she was in DEEP trouble—quicksand trouble!

Chapter 2

Ghost In The Attic?

Addy screamed, "It's Josie!" Turning abruptly, she began running back towards the ear-piercing shouts. I raced past her, knowing the safest places to step. Skye followed quickly behind. We finally reached the edge of 'the desert,' where we needed to carefully trace our steps due to the areas of 'quicksand' from the previous night's rain. From a short distance—maybe a hundred yards, I saw Josie standing still, sinking slowly into the rain-drenched ground.

Still shrieking for help, Addy started running to her. But I stopped her physically, wrenching her arm, and stated desperately, "NO! You don't know where the deep parts are. I'll get to her—just follow my steps."

Addy didn't appear too enthusiastic by my reply. Skye, on the other hand, gave me a look that I interpreted as 'don't worry—I've got her covered.'

As we carefully retraced our steps, I continuously called out to Josie, "Don't worry—we'll be right there."

Josie screamed, "Hurry up, I'm sinking!"

Calmingly, I replied, "We'll be right there, AND you won't sink anymore—it's just wet sand. In fact, it's best if you stop moving around so much. You're just going to dig yourself in deeper."

I didn't have any idea if it were just sand or REAL quicksand, but my instincts told me it would be all right. My dad had never cautioned me about anything like that when we went hiking, and we had spent a lot of time learning about the wilderness.

Shortly after those thoughts, I reached Josie. Addy and Skye were close behind.

I comforted Josie, saying, "It's OK—Look at me, my feet aren't sinking. Grab hold of my hands, lift one foot out, and place it near mine."

Josie looked at Addy in terror, and all Addy could do was nod her head encouragingly. Josie glanced down at her left foot and, holding my hands tightly, proceeded to slowly unhinge her foot from the weighted wet sand. Smiling as her foot popped out with a sucking noise, she placed her mucky shoe next to mine. I grinned and said, "See? It's fine. OK, now the other one."

Confidently, Josie wasted no time in pulling her right foot out. But—in hurrying,—nothing came out but her barefoot! Glancing back in alarm, Josie cried, "Those are my brand-new shoes." With tears spilling down her cheeks, she looked at Addy and sobbed, "Mom's going to kill me."

Skye stepped slightly forward and said assuredly, "Don't worry about that—the three of us will find your shoe." While Skye plunked down on her knees and began digging at the area of Josie's lost shoe, Addy and I looked at one another in concern.

Skye glanced back at us and challenged irritably, "Well—are you two going to help or not?"

As Josie sat a safe distance away with tears still streaming down her face, Addy, Skye, and I dug close to the spot Josie's shoe had disappeared. We kept our distance from the exact place where it had sunk but leaned over far enough to cover the area. We found nothing…

After a half-hour or more, we gave up.

Josie, who was still crying—agreed to go home and face her mother. It was a disappointing and dreadful walk back. First of all, we were going to have to explain to Mrs. Davies what Josie did (and lost). Secondly, Skye, Addy, and I were really ticked off that we didn't get to the 'haunted bus' or the impressive tree fort. Worst of all, for Addy, we never got to collect the tadpoles and plants for her project.

We arrived back at Skye's house just after her mother had gotten home from work. Approaching the house, I asked Skye tentatively, "Shouldn't we try and clean some of this mud off ourselves before we go inside?"

Skye exclaimed, "Yeah—that's definitely a good idea!"

We traipsed, drenched in thick mud to the back of her house, then Skye pulled out their hose and turned the water on. She proceeded to try to spray the muck off our shoes and lower pant legs. Unfortunately, it didn't erase all the evidence… especially because Josie was missing a sneaker and a sock.

Skye looked dismal as she commented, "That's the best I can do. Maybe Josie will dry off a little before she gets home."

Addy replied sarcastically, "Yeah, right—and I'm positive my Mom won't notice Josie's missing shoe!"

Mrs. Finnegan heard the water running and, through the back screen, asked Skye why the water hose was on. Skye answered quickly, "There's no problem, Mom, we just wanted to clean the dirt off our arms before we brought Josie home. We'll be back in a few minutes." We hurried off while Skye yelled back, "We're starving! So, I hope you're making an awesome dinner."

Before we heard Mrs. Finnegan's reply, we walked Josie home. When we entered the house, Josie started crying, even before Mrs. Davies saw her. We tried to explain what happened, but her mother was furious—not that much with us, but with Josie for disobeying her. I really didn't think she was angry at Addy. But just the same, she punished her by saying, "Your sister got into a dangerous situation because she followed you! I know it's not entirely your fault, and I really don't care about the shoe—but she could have gotten lost or worse. Tonight, you'll stay here, clean both of your clothes, cook dinner, and take care of your sister. If you're lucky, you'll be able to go back to Skye's house tomorrow night. Understood?"

Mrs. Davies then looked gravely at Skye and me and said sternly, "If Addy obeys the conditions, then she'll call you tomorrow. If she doesn't, then you won't hear from her, and I'd appreciate it if you don't call or come over."

Skye and I nodded meekly, turned, and left Addy's house. We didn't say much until we were walking up Skye's driveway.

Dismally, I said to Skye, "Well, that was a disaster."

Skye answered shortly, "Yeah, it was. But truthfully, I think it was Josie's fault—not ours, and besides, I'm so hungry that I hope my Mom made something perfect for dinner."

As we entered the house, the incredible aroma of pasta, sauce, and garlic filled our senses. Shortly we saw loaves of bread smothered in butter, garlic, and cheese with angel hair pasta waiting for the somewhat spicy sauce to smother it with. On the table were five settings of dishes, with tasty salads upon each one.

Mr. Finnegan sat at the head of the table and asked perplexed, "Where's Addy? Shouldn't we wait for her?"

Skye answered apprehensively, "She can't stay over tonight. There was a problem with Josie, and Mrs. Davies said she was needed at home to help."

Then trying to sound cheerful, Skye added, "But she'll be back tomorrow night."

We enthusiastically ate our dinner and then afterward went upstairs to the turret room. I looked at the time and exclaimed to Skye, "Wow! It's after ten o'clock, and we didn't stop and take care of my pets!"

Skye, glancing at the clock, replied, amazed, "I can't believe it's that late."

I asked, "Do you think your Mom will be mad if we go back to my house and take care of them?"

Skye answered, "She won't be happy, but she'll be a lot angrier if we don't go. Come on—let's go tell her."

It was like Skye had assumed—her Mom was mad but told us to get going and don't let it happen again.

As soon as we got back to the Turret, Skye said, "Let's get ready for bed, and maybe we'll have time for a short movie."

When we were both ready, I climbed to the top bunk while Skye snuggled into the bottom one below me with the remote. As usual, we picked out a creepy thriller movie, and halfway through, my eyes started drooping. I heard Skye yawning several times. Finally, I asked, "Can we finish this tomorrow? It's terrific, but after everything that happened today, I just can't keep awake any longer."

As a final yawn overtook her, Skye replied, "OK. Night-night." She shut the remote control off, and darkness surrounded us like a shroud.

Sleep overtook us immediately. I slept like the dead until three o'clock in the morning when I awoke to what I thought were footsteps above my bunk bed. I waited a few minutes, thinking I imagined whatever it was I heard.

Then, just as I was falling back asleep, I heard creaking above me again!

My heart was pounding, but I didn't want Skye to wake up and know how frightened I was. I carefully and as silently as possible climbed down the ladder and studied Skye. Not wanting to startle her, I gently rubbed her arm and whispered, "Skye—wake up—Skye…"

Once again, I heard creaking footsteps in the turret attic. I didn't want to scare Skye, so taking a calming breath, I whispered once more, "Skye—wake up."

Groggily, Skye opened her eyes, but sensing something was wrong, she began sitting up with questions perched on her lips.

Desperately, I shook my head 'no' while quickly but gently covered her mouth with my hand. I pointed upwards to the attic and whispered into her ear, "I've heard noises—creaking footsteps, for some time now. Please don't say anything—just listen along with me for a while. Please…"

Skye, eyes wide open—looked upwards, then nodded her head.

I removed my hand, and she moved over towards the wall, then I slipped in next to her. We waited… for something.

Seconds seemed like minutes—but before a few minutes had elapsed, we both heard it, footsteps eerily creeping above us in the attic that supposedly 'wasn't safe.'

Skye and I listened for several more moments as the noises continued. Then with fear overcoming us, we crept as silently as we could out of bed and made our way hurriedly, on tiptoes, out of the room. We raced down the stairs and burst into Mr. and Mrs. Finnegan's room, blurting out, "There's someone in the attic!"

Chapter 5
Questions?

Mr. and Mrs. Finnegan were jarred awake by our outbursts. Sitting up immediately, Mrs. Finnegan yelled out frightfully, "WHAT? WHAT IS IT?"

Mr. Finnegan, while rolling back the covers and slipping quickly into his robe, asked hurriedly but calmly, "What exactly did you hear?"

Skye answered swiftly, "We BOTH heard footsteps in the attic above the turret room, AND we heard them more than once!"

Mrs. Finnegan turned toward us and stopped uncovering the blankets to get up. She tilted her head slightly and asked in an irritated manner, "Were both of you watching scary movies before you went to bed?"

Skye replied instantly, "We weren't dreaming or imagining anything— and if you don't go check it out now, then it might be too late!"

Mr. Finnegan was already leaving the room as his wife shouted, "It's probably just some pigeons!" Aggravated, Skye's mother grabbed her headphones to shut out our chattering as she laid back in her bed. She was probably listening to some soothing Irish music.

Meanwhile, Mr. Finnegan sleepily climbed the turret bedroom steps, while Skye and I followed cautiously behind. Upon reaching the room, Skye's Dad signaled for us to be quiet as he listened vigilantly. The watch on my wrist ticked second by second, but no other sound reached my ears. Even though Mr. Finnegan had climbed onto the top bunk (my bed) and stretched up high enough to lift the attic opening slightly—we heard nothing…

After a final minute or two, Mr. Finnegan closed the gap and stepped down to the floor. Looking at Skye and me, he stated simply, "There's nothing there. Your mother was probably right—too many movies and too much caffeine. It's best that you just go to bed."

Skye raged in astonishment, "ARE YOU SERIOUS?"

Her father, dumbfounded by her intensity, repeated sternly, "It's BEST that you go to bed!"

Skye, although upset, courageously answered her father. "We heard those footsteps, and there's no way we're staying in here tonight. We'll just take our stuff and go to sleep in my room."

Realizing she had never raised her voice to her father like that, she questioned quietly, "If that's OK with you?"

Surprisingly, her father replied, "You can sleep in your room, and I'll check out the attic first thing tomorrow." Sternly, he added, "I don't want to hear any more about it until I've done so—goodnight."

Skye and I rushed to leave the room with our belongings and even brushed past Mr. Finnegan in the stairwell in our haste to reach Skye's bedroom.

Upon reaching Skye's room, she dove quickly into her double bed and pulled the covers up close around her. Still scared of our experience, I asked, "Where should I sleep?"

Skye scrambled out of bed, rushed to her closet, and grabbed two blankets. She tossed them to me and snuggled back into her bed, saying, "Here—use my other pillow and sleep next to me on top of the comforter. You can use the blankets I gave you. She proceeded to scoot to 'her' side of the bed as I lay down and wrapped the blankets tightly around myself. It took us a while to fall asleep, but before we did, I asked Skye, "What do you think Addy would have done if she were here with us?"

Skye chuckled and replied softly, "We'd be halfway to Aruba by now."

Smiling, I whispered, "I wish I WAS in Aruba."

Skye poked me with her elbow and said sarcastically, "Good Night!"

The following morning, we awoke after only a few hours of sleep. Neither of us was in the best of moods when Mrs. Finnegan burst into Skye's room stating irritably, "Skye—I've been yelling for you to pick up the phone! It's Addy." She slammed the door shut as Skye tried to roll over me to get at her phone.

I yelled, "Oomph!" when Skye's sixth-month old puppy, Shuger, jumped onto the bed, and a brief, confusing struggle erupted before I handed her the phone."

Skye asked irritably while pressing the speaker button, "What is it?"

I heard Addy ask cheerfully, "Hey—it's nine o'clock, and I can come over now! What are we doing today?" she added happily. "I can't wait to get out of here."

Skye and I looked at one another, and we both started telling Addy what had happened. Apparently, it came out as a garbled mess because Addy shouted, "STOP! I can't understand anything you're saying."

Skye replied, "Give us a few minutes—we'll call you back."

After hanging up the phone, we calmed ourselves, and I went off to get dressed, while Skye phoned Addy back and gave her a few details of what happened last night. She ended the call by saying we'd meet her outside at ten o'clock.

After getting our clothes on, we went downstairs and found Mrs. Finnegan in the kitchen, putting out our breakfast. Neither of us felt like eating, but we poured out some cereal and milk as Skye's Mom laid out a bowl of assorted fresh fruits. Then looking at Skye, she stated, "I don't want to hear a thing about what you 'think' happened last night. Your father is at work, and when he comes home, he'll check out the attic."

Eyes downcast, Skye just nodded.

We met Addy precisely at ten o'clock, and while walking to my house to take care of my pets, Addy interrupted us a thousand times with questions. After our explanations, she finally understood all of what we had experienced.

Addy paused, concentrating for several moments before I impatiently asked, "Well? What do you think?"

Shaking her head slightly, she replied, "Well, first of all, I'm not sleeping at Skye's house tonight."

Skye and I were outraged! Sheepishly, she added, "At least not until we talk to Mr. Grimly."

Baffled, I asked, "What?"

Addy—who I admit was smarter than Skye and me together, answered, "Mr. Grimly has been here almost his whole life—long before our homes were built. If there's something strange going on at Skye's house, then he's sure to know. Besides, the first owners added that section of the house even after ours were built—so he'd definitely remember anything strange going on since then."

I replied enthusiastically, "Addy—you're a genius!"

Addy smiled triumphantly and asked, "So, when do you want to go visit Mr. Grimly?"

Skye raised her eyebrows and asked sneakily, "Don't we have to take Fluffums, Shugar, and Katie for a walk to see their 'Mom' Puffin?"

Addy and I laughed, knowing that our three, sixth month-old puppies were a gift from Mr. Grimly and his dog Puffin—was our puppy's Mom.

In agreement, we set off to gather our pets and walked towards the 'dreaded' Grimly Manor. Smiling to ourselves, because only a few people knew the truth behind the 'mask,' we weren't afraid.

Upon reaching the ancient manor, we glanced at the exceedingly old cemetery partially surrounding it. Then, we knocked on the newly furnished door. We were surprised as previously we might have banged right through it as decrepit as it had been before.

Mr. Grimly tentatively opened it after gazing through the tiny new peek hole embedded in it. Puffin barked excitedly as the door opened, then Mr. Grimly welcomed us in.

With all the commotion of the three pups and their Mom, it took only a few seconds for me to realize the change in Mr. Grimly. It had been a month or so since I'd seen him, but I couldn't believe my eyes, and neither could Skye or Addy.

I shouted joyously, "Mr. Grimly—YOU'VE GOT LIPS—AND A GREAT NEW CHIN!"

He smiled for the first time with his new features, and we were all laughing tearfully."

He explained to us the efforts that our parents had been going through to help him get his plastic surgery.

"But enough of that for now, what brings you, three lovely ladies, here, besides reuniting these pups with their Mom?"

Blushing, Skye glanced at me to begin.

Chewing my lower lip, I began, "Well—last night, I slept over Skye's house—in the turret room addition." I rambled on about what happened and afterward asked hesitantly, "Were we just hearing things, or is there something more? I know it seems silly, but we were terrified and thought if there was—something to be afraid of—then you might know." Grimacing slightly, I lowered my eyes, waiting for a response.

Mr. Grimly considered his answer for a while. He then replied, "I'm not sure I should tell you any of this but let me make us some lovely tangerine tea with honey while I mull it over."

The three of us went out to give him a hand and carry our cups into the living room.

He sat, stirring his tea, and then said slowly. "This has not been proven, and very few people know about it, so I'll ask you not to say anything you don't have to."

He continued, "But, given the circumstances and my own experiences, I'll say this, the previous owner of your home (looking at Skye), was Mr. Callendish. He committed suicide in the attic above the turret bedroom."

All three of us gasped in horror! But Mr. Grimly waved his hand downwards, then scratched his head and stated sadly, "In my opinion, the truth has never been uncovered. The doctors agreed he died from a heart attack, after slitting his wrists and then hanging himself—but I knew him—and I believe he was murdered."

Chapter 6

Investigation

After Mr. Grimly had uttered the word 'murder,' the three of us pounced on him with a bushel full of questions.

Immediately, he replied calmingly, "Sit down, and I'll tell you what I know."

Excited, terrified, and impatient, we sat down on his sofa, squirming a bit, and tried not to ask questions. Listening intently, we were soon mesmerized by his recounting of the events that happened at Skye's house before the Finnegan's had purchased it.

Mr. Grimly began, "Skye, your home had been for sale for quite some time before your parents bought it. I believe the reason for that was the 'apparent' suicide of the previous owner—Mr. Callendish."

Skye looked slightly mortified at his statement while Addy and I tried to stay composed.

Mr. Grimly continued, "Mr. & Mrs. Callendish first acquired your home a few months after it was built, but Mrs. Callendish didn't seem happy with it."

"Mr. Callendish—'Rupert', was a well-known and highly respected man, who owned a flourishing candy business in Millbrook, NY. He had several small divisions throughout New England, and you might even remember eating one or more of his candies."

Addy interrupted quickly, "Which candies?"

Skye and I waited expectantly for his reply.

Smiling, Mr. Grimly questioned. "Have you ever had Christmas Crinkles, Choco-Peanutters, Grape Gushers, or Strawberry Blasts? They were the most popular as I recall."

Ghost in the Turret

The three of us nodded enthusiastically, and I replied astounded, "Mr. Callendish was THAT Mr. Callendish—the one who made those candies?"

He replied, nodding, "Yes—that—Mr. Callendish."

Mr. Grimly continued, "After Rupert had purchased your house, Skye, he began construction on an addition. He was there as much as possible, overseeing the add-ons. Despite my neighborhood reputation and disfigurement, we eventually became casual friends. Rupert was a quiet man and didn't talk much about his wife, other than to say that she wouldn't be arriving until the renovations were complete."

"I should probably add that he was a wealthy man and apparently wanted to make his wife happy."

"Anyway, after the new turreted addition was finished, 'SHE—Evelyn' came to live there. I asked Rupert just once, what the importance of the added rooms was, and he shook his head slowly and replied, "Truthfully, Albert, I have no idea. I just give Evelyn whatever makes her happy. But actually, I made some changes for my own reasons. Maybe she just wants a room she can call her own or some fancy dream room. Right now, I honestly don't know."

Skye, Addy, and I waited patiently for Mr. Grimly to continue.

He sighed, and then seemingly shaking cobwebs out of his head, asked, "Do any of you girls want any more refreshment?"

Skye perked up immediately and replied, "Yes! After the hot tea, I think something cold would be great!"

Skye was longing to see where he kept his cold items.

She added a quick, "Thank you."

Skye and I offered to help as we followed him through the kitchen and down into the root cellar, where he kept his cold storage. He didn't have electricity, but we had learned how he managed and why through the past eight months. It was the first time we had actually seen the old root cellar, and although it was slightly eerie, we weren't afraid. He grabbed a few bottles of fresh-squeezed lemonade, and we followed him back to the kitchen, where he poured out four glasses. Winking at us, with a smile, he said, "It's homemade, and you'll never taste any better."

Settling back down into the sofa, we sipped our drinks. As the lemonade flowed past our taste buds, we each let out different sounds of appreciation. Mr. Grimly glanced upward, smiling in contentment, and continued with his insight into the mysterious happenings at Skye's reasonably new home.

Savoring his lemonade, Mr. Grimly thought carefully before continuing his story. "Well, since Rupert and I had become acquainted, it seemed obvious to me that Evelyn still wasn't entirely happy with her new home. Rupert was often away for the Candy factory business. But Evelyn—who didn't make any friends in the neighborhood, became what I'd call 'waspish.' Eventually, no one wanted to speak to her."

"Leira—you might remember her—even though you were still very young."

Squinting, I searched back through my memories and then tentatively replied, "I think I do, but just vaguely. Mrs. Callendish always frightened me. The worst thing I recall is that her eyes seemed black as coal and full of anger when she looked at me. I just barely remember that whenever I did see her, I ran back inside my house."

Perplexed, I added, "I don't think I've even thought about her until now."

"Well, replied Mr. Grimly, I don't doubt that you would have been frightened by her. Sometimes, I think that Rupert stayed away on business just to keep away from her."

He continued, "Anyway, after a few years, I noticed Rupert was much more nervous and staying away for more extended periods. I asked him about it one day, and he said that the business was picking up, and he needed to be away longer. I inquired how Evelyn was dealing with his absence."

"He answered anxiously that she was secluding herself in her newly added room. He also said he had no idea what she was doing. Still, he did mention that she kept a laptop, phone, and accounting material, which he ran across one day when the door was open."

"She explained that she was doing some work for a travel agency and would be taking a few trips to check on locations."

Skye questioned exuberantly, "And did she? Work for a travel agency? Why would that have anything to do with the attic of the turret room?"

Mr. Grimly replied apprehensively, "Skye, I honestly have no idea. I was never included in any neighborhood gatherings or information." Sadly, he added, "Maybe she did. I can only tell you what Rupert told me. I don't know how this comes together, but your parents might have an idea or two."

"Honestly, I can't say that what she was working on had anything to do with the turret addition. I can tell you this though, Rupert LOVED to paint, which is why he changed the addition. It was so he could go up into the attic in the morning (while she was still sleeping) and paint while the morning sun came up in the east."

A brief silence occurred before I asked Mr. Grimly gravely, "What do you think happened in that attic? The police said it was suicide, but you think it was murder."

Mr. Grimly eyed me intensely, then replied, "I believe Rupert was murdered. It was not in his character to slash his wrists or hang himself, even with that evil woman pushing him to the edge. But his death has been ruled a suicide. So, she inherited all the money from his businesses, and the house was finally sold. Evelyn has moved, and Rupert is buried in the cemetery behind my home—the last to be buried there."

Addy erupted me out of my deep thoughts, stating, "Leira, we've got to be back at Skye's house for lunch."

Thanking Mr. Grimly for confiding in us, we called our dogs, Fluffums, Katie, and Shugar. After gathering them up, we left Grimly Manor, but not before searching out the grave of Mr. Rupert Callendish.

While standing at the headstone, I stated firmly, "I believe Mr. Grimly. I think his crazy wife murdered him. I think we should go to the library and dig up any information we can on what happened." Glancing at Skye and Addy, they both agreed. So, we headed back to my house to drop off Fluffums and take care of my other my pets while Addy brought Katie home. We met up shortly afterward before returning to Skye's house.

After having tuna sandwiches with chips and Grape Seltzer for lunch, I suggested, "Why don't we go to the library and find out everything we can about Mr. Callendish's suicide? That must have been big news at that time. What do you think?"

Addy and Skye agreed immediately, and after finishing our lunch, we walked the half-mile to the public library. We were getting surprisingly good at utilizing the library resources. Without any help, we soon found the old articles related to the suicide of Mr. Callendish.

Nothing we read seemed to add up. Mr. Callendish had bought his wife's dream house, made the additions she wanted, and, as far as anyone knew, was a devoted husband.

So—our burning question was—why did he kill himself, or—did something more sinister happen in Skye's home?

We continued to pull out books relating to the construction of our homes, the death of Mr. Callendish, the whereabouts of Evelyn Callendish, and what happened to 'Callendish Candies.'

After our investigating was finished for the day, we walked back to Skye's house.

Exhausted, we plunked down in the living room. Skye got up slowly and said, "I'll get some drinks and snacks."

Standing up, I replied, "I'll help." Skye nodded thankfully as Addy gazed out the window considering what could be done next.

Returning shortly, we sipped our drinks, thinking the same thing—what's the next step?

Looking at Skye, I enquired, "Where do you want to sleep tonight?"

Fearfully, Addy suggested, "Maybe we should sleep in your room tonight—at least until we know more about what happened."

Skye chewing on her lips, finally replied, "I guess one more night in my room is Okay. But we need to talk about everything we've figured out until now."

I nodded my head in agreement and asked, "What will you tell your parents?"

Shrugging her shoulders, she answered, "I don't think they'll care, as long as we don't make too much noise."

Awkwardly, we readied ourselves for bed as Skye told her parents she was getting a movie and that we were going to sleep in her room.

Mrs. Finnegan asked Skye, "Are you afraid of spending the night in the 'special' guest room?"

Skye answered, "The three of us feel a little uneasy, and we want to get a good night's sleep after last night."

Mrs. Finnegan said, "It's OK. I understand."

Skye had a double-sized bed with a trundle pull out, so I slept with Skye, and Addy used the trundle bed. We murmured for a few hours about what we had learned and what we should do next.

It was past midnight when I barely heard something moving. It seemed to be coming from the roof or the attic of the turret. I nudged Skye and groaning, she asked groggily, "What?"

I replied quietly, "Listen—do you hear that noise?"

Skye was silent for several seconds before replying irritably, "No, I don't hear anything—and I'm really sleepy, so let me go back to dreaming."

I listened for a while afterward, but eventually, sleep captured me.

Chapter 7
Mysterious Intruder

It wasn't long after falling into an uneasy sleep that I awoke to another noise coming from upstairs. I wasn't sure if it was the turret room or the attic above. In my state of drowsiness, I couldn't tell. Becoming fully awake while continuing to strain my ears for more sounds, I scarcely heard the creaking steps just above the window outside Skye's bed. I nudged her softly, gently covering her mouth as she quickly awakened. Pressing my finger to my lips, I whispered, "Listen."

Suddenly awake and with eyes wide open, she strained to hear. Within seconds, we both listened to another creak! To me, it seemed a little higher up, but Skye heard it too.

Softly, Skye whispered, "Shouldn't we wake Addy?"

I quickly shook my head no, then suggested softly, "Let's go up to the turret room and peek out through the window."

We listened intently once again and heard more creaking 'footsteps' further up.

I urged quickly but quietly, "Let's go."

Skye, nodding in agreement, tiptoed immediately up the steps behind me and into the Turret room. Then, we cautiously pulled back the curtain covering the window and peered out. We carefully looked for something—anything; A ghost, spirit, whatever… We didn't know anything other than we were facing a terrible fear—not even knowing what it was!

Horrified, we heard another scrape above us, which meant whatever or whoever was there was attempting to enter the attic above the turret. Terrified, we decided to open the guest room window and look for the source. After soundlessly raising the window, we poked our heads out and looked upwards. Much to our horror, we saw a figure standing on a ladder, who seemed to be trying to open the small attic window. Stricken with terror, we glanced at one another. Before I could ask Skye what she wanted to do, Addy burst into the room—flipping on the lights—demanding to know why we had left her all alone. Sensing the tension building up, she raced to the window and looked outside, then upwards. Gasping, she backed up and yelled, "Help me push that ladder over NOW!"

Horrified that she had turned on the lights, we realized that the intruder now knew we were there. But the demand emanating from Addy caused Skye and me to quickly help Addy grab the ladder and push outwards with all our strength. We didn't stop to think that if it was a ghost that it would just disappear, but if it were a person, then they could be severely injured or even DIE! Our only thought was about getting rid of the 'curse' or 'spirits' haunting Skye's' home.

An agonizing scream resounded as the ladder fell backward, frightening us in several ways. Addy raced to the window to join us, just as the ladder slammed against the old oak tree several feet away. A figure, whose screams chilled us, remained glued to the ladder a few feet below where it hit a tree.

Each of us strained to see the person—or apparition still clinging to its perch. Finally, Addy called out uncertainly, "Jeffrey? Is that you?"

Skye and I were stunned, and I quickly whispered to Addy, "Do you really think it's Jeffrey?"

My answer came shortly—not from Addy, but from Jeffrey.

"Of course, it's me, you idiots! This ladder is pegging me against this stupid tree. I know you're probably angry right now, but I really need some help to get down."

Addy looked skeptically at Skye and me, then raising her brows, questioned quietly, "Well? Should we go help—or let him suffer?"

Both Skye and I wanted to let him 'suffer' for a while. But finally, I replied, "We'd better go help him and find out why he's here, or there might be more questions from our parents than we want to answer."

Immediately, Skye, wide-eyed, and then Addy both nodded in agreement, and we rushed (quietly) downstairs and outside to help Jeffrey get down.

"Good grief, Jeffrey Kuvasc!" Addy scolded. "What on Earth do you think you were doing—other than almost getting yourself killed or crippled?"

Jeffrey carefully climbed down the ladder, humbled by his humiliation, but managed to tell Addy, "I was worried about you and all the rumors that have been going around." Embarrassed, he glanced down while shuffling the dirt around his feet.

Skye pounced on him like a vicious cat, "And just what 'rumors' would you know about?"

Jeffrey gulped and took a step backward at the sight of Skye's fury, and answered softly, but sincerely, "I've heard several things since I moved here a few months ago. The first thing I heard was that your house was haunted, and you might be moving."

Skye gave Jeffrey a furious look that paused him for a moment. But he took a deep breath and continued, "I've also heard rumors about 'the desert, the old bones, the quicksand, the ancient treehouse, and the old, haunted bus."

Glancing at each of us one at a time, he then added, "I'd like to help you solve the Mystery's—or at least—help protect you."

Jeffrey added, "Before you say no, I want you to know that I really want to help you find out whatever happened in the attic of Skye's turret room! AND I'm not afraid to do whatever it takes to find the culprit behind it."

Addy challenged, "Even if it's a ghost?"

Jeffrey replied bravely, "Even—if it's a ghost!"

After a lengthy pause, I replied suspiciously, "Well, they're probably is a ghost, but the unknown will probably be worse—are you ready for that too?"

Jeffrey—wanting to be a hero in Addy's mind, said, "Of course. I'll be there to protect all of you."

Containing my laughter, while glancing at Skye, I replied, "Okay. We can always use another team member."

Continuing, I added, "Tomorrow, I think we should all go to Mr. Grimly's house and ask him what else he knows about Skye's house. I'm sure we'll be able to gather a bunch of information to help us."

Looking directly at Jeffrey, I asked pointedly, "Are you going with us?"

Jeffrey, looking as though he'd been punched in the chest, answering bravely (while looking at Addy), "Of course I'll go." Somehow, his reply didn't come across as sincere as he intended.

But Addy smiled appreciatively and said to all of us (Jeffrey included), "It's settled then. We'll go back to see Mr. Grimly tomorrow and find out what more he knows."

Addy glanced quickly but cheerfully at Jeffrey, just before he stated, "I'm really going to be in trouble if I don't get back to my home and sneak back in. So, I'd better get going, and I'll see you tomorrow." Turning, he rapidly jogged back to his house while the rest of us re-entered Skye's home.

I couldn't help but take one last glance at Jeffrey. His urgency and exuberance seemed to be something of a person who was experiencing embarrassment and happiness at the same time.

It was almost four o'clock in the morning, and Skye suggested that we take care of my pets while we were all up, so we didn't have to get up early. Addy volunteered to come with me, while Skye said, "I'll stay behind to answer any questions from my parents if they wake up before you return."

I didn't have much time to consider anything while Addy and I entered my house. My dog Lucky was barking/howling for food. My puppy Fluffums was 'attacking me' for food and play, and my sweet cat Emmy was sitting pitifully next to her food bowl (which was empty) meowing at me.

Our house seemed eerily quiet without my parents' home. Still, I almost sensed a chill of their presence, making sure I was taking care of my pets, or there would be a severe punishment upon their return.

As tired as we were, Addy and I took care of all three of 'my babies,' then exhausted, walked back to Skye's house.

Donna Wren Carson

    Snuggling into my half of the bed and drifting off to sleep, I thought I heard my Mom ask, "Did you take care of your pets?"
    I replied sleepily, "Yes, I did. Night… night."
    Dreaming, I heard my Mom reply, "Night-Night Pudding Pie…"

Chapter 8

A New Accomplice

Surprisingly, Addy was the first one awake, and she rudely shook me while barking, "WAKE UP!"

Groggily, I turned over and opened my eyes slightly as the sun was beaming brightly through the windows. Exhausted, I asked quietly, "What's going on? What time is it?"

Annoyed, Addy responded, "It's TEN O'clock in the morning, and Mr. and Mrs. Finnegan have been trying to get you guys up for 2 HOURS! I've only gotten three or four hours of sleep, and it's time YOU GUYS were up!"

Even though I was still half asleep, I began to understand Addy's annoyance from lack of sleep. Calmly, I replied to Addy, "OK, I'll wake Skye—you get dressed. By the way, don't forget we're going to see Mr. Grimly today." Addy shot back a look of disdain before marching off to the bathroom.

Gently, I woke Skye, even though she wasn't very enthusiastic about it. As she sleepily sat up, I softly punched her in the arm. As she turned angrily to retort, I said, "Just pretend we're in the desert with Luke on our last adventure, and there's nothing to eat but cactus!"

I smiled then, as Skye recalled the moment that had really happened during our winter vacation in Arizona, and we both burst out laughing! In fact, we couldn't stop laughing. Our present situation was so less frightening because we were home.

During our outbreak of hysterics, Addy re-entered the room and looked at us with complete outrage. Neither of us could possibly re-create our connection that led to our outburst, but, stifling the last of my chuckles, I said, "Sorry, Addy. We're just exhausted and began laughing about parts of our 'Adventure in Arizona.'"

Just then, Mrs. Finnegan knocked on the door, and before we could reply, she stepped into the room. She firmly stated (but with a hint of pride), "I've spent the last hour making apple-fritter French toast, scrambled eggs, crispy smoked bacon, and fresh-squeezed orange juice. If you don't get downstairs in three minutes, I'm going to eat my fill and feed the rest of it to your dogs."

Swiftly, turning her back to us (but not before I saw a glint of amusement in her eyes), she marched back down the stairs.

Skye glanced quickly at Addy and me and exclaimed, "Hurry up, or you won't get any!"

Addy and I followed as quickly as possible, only stopping to throw on our robes and slippers. After the night we had just experienced, we needed as much nourishment as we could get—not to mention how delicious it sounded and smelled!

After devouring our food, Mrs. Finnegan re-entered the kitchen. She announced flippantly, "Oh, and by the way, Skye, make sure you and your friends put away the leftovers and wash the dishes." Turning her back, she left the room, and Skye grimaced before saying, "Sorry about that. She's just mad that we were up so late."

Addy smirked and replied, "Well, I won't get into trouble if I curl up in front of the TV while you guys clean up the mess. I wasn't the one who got up late!"

Skye walked a few steps towards Addy, and when they were face to face, she tilted her head downwards a bit, squinting, and said, "I don't care WHO got up first. You're part of our team, and you'll HELP! Understand?"

I'd rarely seen Skye so upset, but Addy immediately nodded her head in acknowledgment, and the three of us polished off the job in minutes. Addy and Skye never muttered a word, but in the back of her mind, Addy recalled, "Hmm, I thought Jeffrey was part of our team."

Afterward, I suggested, "Let's get dressed, then go and see Mr. Grimly. I'm sure he'll know something more about what happened here and if there's really a ghost."

Skye reminded us quickly, "Don't forget that Jeffrey's coming with us. So… who's going to call him?" Skye looked at Addy for a reply.

I smothered a grin, while Addy replied indignantly, "Well, I'm not going to call him! Besides, I don't have his phone number."

Skye smirked and said, "Well, I do." She handed the paper with Jeffrey's number on it to Addy along with the phone, then said sternly, "Dial!"

Addy asked quickly, "How did you get this?" She cringed at the tone of Skye's voice when she replied, "Ever heard of the internet?"

Addy gulped and reluctantly dialed Jeffrey's number. When his mother answered, she paused slightly before stuttering, "Is Jeffrey there?"

His mother questioned, "Whose calling?"

Addy answered embarrassingly, "Addy Davies."

His Mom replied, "Oh! I've heard so many nice things about you. He's downstairs; I'll get him for you."

While Jeffrey's Mom left to get him, we pressed the speakerphone button, so when he answered, the three of us could hear the conversation.

Jeffrey sounded enthusiastic when he answered. Happily, he said, "Hi, Addy! Can I help you with anything?"

Addy took a deep, slow breath before replying, "Well yes, Jeffrey—actually, you could do a big favor for my friends and me."

Interrupting, he asked, "You mean Leira and Skye—don't you?"

Addy acknowledged his suspicion but explained. "We want the three of us—well four—including you, to go over to Mr. Grimly's house and ask more questions about the previous owners' of Skye's house. The three of us get the impression that he has a lot more information than he's told us, and we want you to come along."

There was a long pause on the other end of the phone, and Addy asked, "Jeffrey? Are you still there?"

A moment later, Jeffrey replied, "Yep, ah—what time did you want to go?"

Addy replied, "Well, Mr. Grimly doesn't have a phone, so we can't call and ask. But I think noon would be good. We could bring him some lunch." Hesitating, because Jeffrey hadn't made a sound, she asked, "Does that sound OK to you?"

After a moment, Jeffrey replied, "Hey, I need to go home for lunch, so that's not a good time. Why don't you guys go over and let me know what's going on afterward."

Addy angrily asked, "Jeffrey Kuvasc! Are you afraid again? If you are, then you're not the person I thought you were! The three of us will do simply fine without any help from you!"

As Addy was about to slam the phone down, I held her hand, and we heard Jeffrey rapidly reply, "I'm not afraid of anything! So—noon will be fine—but make sure you bring enough food for five! I'll be waiting outside for you three to show up."

After that, all three of us heard the phone slam down. Glancing at one another for a few seconds, grins crept onto our faces, then smiles, then chuckles, then all-out laughter.

It was a delightful moment to savor. Jeffrey Kuvasc turned out to be one of many things. He was an ordinary person (afraid of the unknown). And a friend (because he had a big crush on Addy). Lastly—he was courageous (because he conquered his fears to help Addy).

I think all of us learned something special today.

Skye told Mrs. Finnegan that we wanted to make sandwiches for lunch and bring them to Mr. Grimly's so we could all have lunch together.

Mrs. Finnegan slyly asked, "You guys just ate less than two hours ago. Why are you so hungry now?"

Skye replied, "Well, you know Mr. Grimly, he'll have us there for two or three hours. So, I think it's best to bring over some sandwiches and chips. Is that OK?"

Mrs. Finnegan questioned, "And who is the fifth sandwich for?"

Skye replied quickly, "Jeffrey is coming with us to meet Mr. Grimly."

Mrs. Finnegan answered, "Well, that's unexpected. Okay, but, as long as you make them yourselves and be home by 5:30 for dinner."

Skye smiled and said, "No problem."

We spent the next forty-five minutes putting together a lunch for the five of us. We made two peanut butter and jelly sandwiches, one fluffernutter, one ham and cheese on rye bread, and one turkey, cheddar, and lettuce on white bread. We grabbed a new bag of potato chips from the cupboard and put everything in a backpack, along with five bottles of cold spring water. Then we headed over to Jeffrey's house.

Just as promised, he was waiting outside. As we approached, he shuffled his feet, glancing up at Addy every few seconds. He knew he had to make peace with Skye and me if he was ever going to be good friends with Addy. So, as we approached, he asked Skye (who was shouldering the backpack), "Can I carry that for you, Skye?" Skye grinned and replied,

"Thank you, Jeffrey—that would be very nice."

After Jeffrey took the pack, the four of us set off to Mr. Grimly's house. I could see little beads of sweat pop out on Jeffrey's forehead—but I didn't say a thing.

We approached Mr. Grimly's front door with Jeffrey hanging back behind us and proceeded to knock exuberantly. It wasn't necessary because we could hear Puffin barking long before we traipsed up the steps.

Jeffrey, who didn't know about Mr. Grimly and Puffin's history, was very edgy about proceeding. But noticing how happy Addy, Skye, and I were—he just put on a good face and waited.

The door opened quickly, and we were 'attacked' by Mr. Grimly's dog Puffin. After bowling us over with slobbery licks, she smelled around searching for her 'babies,' but we hadn't brought them. Sensing her sadness, I pulled two bacon treats out of my pocket, and she immediately forgot about anything but the tasty treats in my hand.

Lovingly, I handed her one, then made her sit and shake hands for the other.

Mr. Grimly smiled and welcomed us.

Jeffrey just stared at the man before him...

At once, I saw discomfort on Mr. Grimly's disfigured face and whipped my head around to see Jeffrey's shock.

Quickly, I turned back to Mr. Grimly and said, "Mr. Grimly, we're so happy you're home." Extending an arm towards Jeffrey, I continued, "I'd like you to meet our new friend Jeffrey we told you about yesterday. He is going to be helping us to figure out what is happening at Skye's home."

Mr. Grimly looked at Jeffrey apprehensively, and finally said, "Hello Jeffrey. I've seen you out and about since you have moved into the neighborhood."

Jeffrey's face turned a bit ashen, thinking of the bad reputation that had always followed him. Bravely, he stepped forward and reached out a hand to shake Mr. Grimly's.

Smiling a bit, Mr. Grimly reached out and shook Jeffrey's hand. The tension drained away.

I cheerfully said. "Mr. Grimly, we've brought you lunch! So, I hope you are hungry—if not, then Puffin will be getting fat!"

Mr. Grimly replied, "We can't have that. Bring yourselves and your food in, and let's eat."

After settling ourselves in, eating our lunches, and making small talk, Mr. Grimly asked, "So what is the REAL reason for your visit?"

Addy indignantly replied, "What do you mean—the REAL reason? Since when do we need a reason for wanting to see you?"

Mr. Grimly shook his head slightly. Then, he looked into Addy's eyes and asked, "Since when do you bring a new 'friend' with you and not even bring the pups as you always have?"

I spoke up while Mr. Grimly's eyes turned to fasten on me; I intensely but softly said, "Since we know that Skye's house is being haunted by ghosts."

Sternly and steely-eyed, Mr. Grimly replied, "I've already told you there are NO ghosts."

Chapter 9
Another Night In The Turret

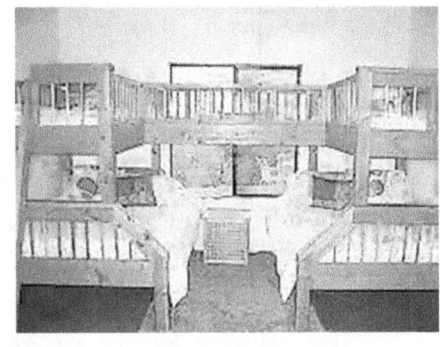

Mr. Grimly stated again, sternly, "There are no ghosts haunting your home Skye Finnegan! All of you need to understand is that whatever happened before has nothing to do with what you think is happening now."

Skye interrupted a bit angrily, "What we 'THINK' is happening now? YOU haven't heard the footsteps that Leira and I have! You haven't been there when we almost fainted in fear to go back a second time and listened to the floorboards creak over and again. AND it wasn't Jeffrey in the attic trying to scare us! He was hanging onto a tree for dear life, pinned by the ladder we had pushed over. Luckily, we figured out how to rescue him!"

Mr. Grimly tried to calm Skye. "No, I wasn't there, but from what you've told me now, and with such emotion—." Mr. Grimly paused as his head dipped a bit downward. Images of us saving Jeffrey squashed between a ladder and a tree were almost too much to hide. He continued, "I believe you, and I'll do everything I can to help you solve this mystery or puzzle or whatever you want to call it. I'll be there for you."

At that moment, Puffin came racing into the room, carrying a squeaky toy and jumped up onto my lap!

After suppressing his laughter, Mr. Grimly slowly lifted himself out of his favorite chair, approached Skye, kneeled beside her, and placed his gentle but scarred hands on her shoulders. He looked into her eyes, sympathetically, and shook his head in sorrow. Then, he replied with the slightest glistening of tears in his eyes, "I know what it's like to be afraid—afraid of losing everyone and everything you love. I know you are scared. I also believe that whatever is happening in your home, you have not imagined. And…for that reason, I promise I am going to help you through this and make sure that every one of you is safe. I think we have an incredibly good, new partner who will help us do that." He gave a quick glance toward Jeffrey. "So, for now—don't worry. Together we will figure out what is going on. OK?"

Skye, taking a deep breath, glanced around the room. Looking at Addy, me, Mr. Grimly, and Jeffrey, then back into Mr. Grimly's eyes, she grinned slightly and asked, "OK—so what's the next step?"

Mr. Grimly replied simply, "It's elementary, my dear Skye."

Skye looked utterly confused, then turned to me and murmured, "What does that mean?"

Understandably, I doubted Skye had ever seen any 'Sherlock Holmes' movies, which my dad and I had seen several of. So, I replied, "It's a saying from old movies. It means, 'It's simple,' Skye."

Skye turned towards Mr. Grimly and asked in frustration, "Would you mind telling me the 'simple' part?"

Mr. Grimly smiled (and we all loved to see him smile now). Then, he answered Skye, "You'll have to go back to the Turret room tonight and write down and take pictures of everything you see and hear that is not normal. Can you do that?"

Surprisingly, Jeffrey chose that moment to speak up. He stated, "I'm going to spend the night right outside the room. There's plenty of space in that old tree for me to set myself up comfortably. So, if anything happens, I'll be right there to help."

I couldn't believe what I had just heard, and neither could Addy or Skye.

Skye, exasperated, but appreciative said, "Jeffrey—if you can accomplish that without getting into trouble with your parents, then—thank you."

Jeffrey briefly locked eyes with Addy, and they both gave one another a slight smile.

Skye re-directed the conversation back to Mr. Grimly. She asked him apprehensively, "So what do you think we'll have pictures to take of? We can definitely take notes of strange things happening, but we've been too frightened to stay up there when something weird is going on. So, what do you think we should do to keep ourselves from being afraid?"

Mr. Grimly replied sternly, "Bravery! I know you all possess it! Just get on over there, watch a movie (on low volume) and listen for clues. Jeffrey will be right outside. Your parents Skye will be just below you, and nothing bad will happen. So—go do it. I know you can."

We left Mr. Grimly's mansion and quietly walked for a while, before Jeffrey asked, "So what happened to Mr. Grimly to make him so disfigured?"

Skye, Addy, and I looked at one another, and Addy started to laugh. Jeffrey looked perplexed. Then, Addy stated, "Well, I guess you'll have to read my journal or our minds before we tell you that."

Jeffrey, not wanting to irritate Addy, responded, "Well, when you're ready to confide in me, I'll keep it a secret—promise."

Addy replied, "Well, if Skye and Leira agree, we'll let you know."

Jeffrey nodded his head, encouraged that he would be let in on the secret details.

When we finally reached Jeffrey's home, he gave a last glance at Addy, then asked, "What about that Indian guy you met in Arizona? Have you heard from him?"

Addy gave Jeffrey a look of 'Don't go there,' but graciously replied, "He's been in touch—but—it's really none of your business."

Addy turned around and kept walking to her home next door.

I noticed Jeffrey seemed a bit jealous at her response as his head lowered while walking up to his driveway.

Skye lightened up the situation by reminding us that we would be spending another eventful night with her after we took care of my pets.

I thought to myself, "Eventful could be an incredibly good thing or really awful."

All of us agreed to find the courage and spend the night in the Turret. Just as we had faced frightening situations in the past—we were not going to chicken out now. Besides, the most important thing was that Skye didn't move away.

So, after taking care of Lucky, Fluffums, and Emmy, we headed back over Skye's and up into the turret room. We were all starved, so

Skye made her 'room service' call to her Mom to order our favorite Chinese food.

I only liked the chicken fingers and beef teriyaki, but Addy and Skye wolfed down things I had trouble pronouncing. Skye had Moo Shu Pork (with 5 Pancakes) and white rice. Addy had General Tso's chicken, also with white rice.

Addy's looked and smelled pretty good, so I tried some. It was deep-fried chicken with a sweet but spicy orange sauce covering it. I actually enjoyed it!

We chose a funny movie to watch, and after the events of the day, we were all ready to crawl into bed and go to sleep.

It was almost 11:30, and the three of us fell asleep almost at once.

Then, I woke up abruptly by strange noises and creaking floorboards above me! My heart hammered furiously in my chest, and while I closed my eyes and tried to relax my body, I thought, "This can't really be happening."

After I had composed myself, I whispered to Skye and Addy, "Did either of you hear that?"

At once, they both softly responded, "Yes."

Tentatively, I replied, "What do you think we should do?"

Skye replied, "Let's go sleep in my room, and tomorrow take a trip to the library!"

Addy responded, "Brilliant idea… but let's let Jeffrey know, so he doesn't stay in the tree all night.

"Wait!" I said. "We told Jeffrey and Mr. Grimly that we were going to do this!"

"Now, after one scare, we aren't even checking it out! I think that's terrible. We should at least take some pictures and write down what we've heard—don't you think?"

Addy said, "You're right. We are a bunch of fraidy-cats if we don't do more. I'm going outside and see if Jeffrey is alright and find out if he heard anything."

Skye replied, "Well, you're not going without me. I'm not going to let you go alone."

They both looked at me for my thoughts.

I said, "I'm not so sure that I want to be left here alone, and I'll worry about you guys. But, if I hear anything from upstairs, I'll double flash the lights and either call your parents or run and get them."

"Does that sound like a good plan?"

Cautiously, Addy and Skye agreed, then with baseball bats in hand, they headed outdoors.

I stayed next to the window while listening for anything suspicious. I saw Skye and Addy reach Jeffrey, and it looked like they had to shake him awake. They didn't stay long and soon headed back towards the turret.

When they finally arrived, I blurted out, "What happened?"

Skye snorted and replied, "He fell asleep and didn't hear a thing."

Addy quickly asked me, "Did you hear or see anything weird, Leira?" I said, "No. It's really late. Why don't you send Jeffrey home, and we can write down what we heard as promised? We should leave out the part where Jeffrey fell asleep, or he won't want to try and help anymore."

We all agreed, then at 5:00 am, we finally fell asleep. We woke up really late, and in the morning, after dodging Mrs. Finnegan's questions, we asked her for a ride to the Library to work on school projects. She didn't mind, but she was somewhat suspicious as she dropped us off.

We spent several hours going through old newspaper articles trying to find out about Skye's home. Finally, I found a 'Gold Strike'!

Addy and Skye, hearing my stifled piercing scream of discovery, raced over to see what I had found. It was an article about Skye's home. The previous owner, Mr. Callendish, had been found dead in the turret room's attic!

Chapter 10
The Confrontation

In the Library, after rushing to my side, the three of us read the article I had found about the death of Mr. Callendish. He had been discovered dead in the attic of the Turret room of Skye's home. There were so many unanswered questions from the article that we didn't quite know what to make of it.

I turned to my friends (most directly at Skye), and asked, "Do you think your parents know more than they want to tell us?"

Skye replied irritably, "My mother wouldn't have converted that room into a special guest room if she knew about this. AND have us all stay there if she thought something bad or 'weird' would happen to any of us!"

I answered quickly, "I'm sorry, I didn't mean to make you mad. I just wondered if your parents knew more about the house and didn't want to frighten us. I think I would be a bit freaked out about living in a house where someone had died. I know more people could care less—but I would be creeped out."

Skye replied after thinking about it for a moment or two. "I'm sure they must have known about his death. I think the people who sell houses have to tell the people interested in buying it that kind of stuff."

Skye added, "I imagine that they didn't tell us because they were worried about causing just that reaction."

Skye continued, "I don't really care about that, but I do care about the noises we heard, AND I agree with Mr. Grimly that there are NO ghosts. So, I think there is 'someone' out there who IS trying to frighten us and make us leave, although I don't think my parents would listen to me."

Skye continued, "Either way, something is going on, and I'm going to find out what it is—with or without your help!"

I replied, "Skye, Addy, and I are here to help you solve this mystery, no matter what." Turning to Addy, I waited for her confirmation, which she immediately gave with a quick nod of her head.

Skye said, "I think we should go back to my house, and if both my parents are home, we should confront them and find out what they know. Are you both coming with me?"

I replied immediately, "Absolutely!"

Addy added as I finished, "You bet! Let's go!"

Skye called home, and her ornery brother Liam answered. Skye asked Liam to talk to one of their parents, but he said sarcastically, "Sorry, Sis— they're not home. I guess you'll have to walk home from the Library."

Skye, trying to keep her anger under control, asked, "Hey, I thought you were spending your vacation at your friend's house?" Sweetly, she continued, "I guess Mom and Dad know you're home." She waited for his reply, assuming that her parents didn't know.

"Anyway, we're at the library, and since Mom isn't home, could you pick us up? It's only a mile away."

Liam hesitated and then replied, "I guess I could do that. Only, as long as you and your friends clean the windows of my car when you get back—and don't leave any streaks on it, or you'll never get another favor from me—understood?"

Skye told us his conditions. So, it was a one-mile walk back home or get a ride and clean Liam's car windows. The three of us decided we'd rather clean his car windows—besides, there were three of us—how long could it take?

Although it was already April, the sun quickly disappeared from the sky as thunderheads rolled in. We were glad we made the decision to have Liam pick us up. Ten minutes later, when we thought he would have shown up, a brief flash of lightning lit the sky, and thunder followed a few seconds later.

I said to my friends, "I hope he gets here soon."

Thankfully, we saw his car drive down the library road and ran out to meet him just as the rain started to come down.

We scrambled into his 'hot rod, stick shift' car, and Skye asked, "What took you so long?"

Liam almost sneered as he replied, "The car needed some adjustments. You're just lucky I'm here at all!"

He sped off around the back of the library and onto the main street. The rain became much heavier, and the lightning tore through the clouds as the deafening thunder followed closely.

About a half-mile from Skye's house, the car stalled, and Liam grunted as he smashed his fist on the dashboard.

With the whipping rain becoming more intense and the thunder and lightning more fierce and rapid, Skye loudly asked Liam, "Is there anything we can do?"

Liam replied angrily, "NO! There isn't anything YOU can do. Hopefully, if the rain lessens and the engine isn't flooded, then we should be able to get home." Sarcastically he added, "Unless you want to walk the rest of the way yourself."

Just then, the most brilliant trilogy of lightning flashed, with thunder resounding on top of it. The tree we were stalled next to split in two, and half of it came crashing down just behind Liam's car. It caught on a power line that snapped in two and then started twisting and flinging itself around like a tortured creature.

Liam stated in all seriousness, "Don't any of you move—not an inch!" We gazed at him without moving a muscle to let him know we understood.

He used his cell phone and dialed 911. The emergency crews showed up quickly and rendered the power cable inactive while they proceeded to do their repairs. One of the officers in charge said to Liam, "You did the right thing, kid." Glancing at the three of us in the back seat, he continued, "You and your friends might not have been around tomorrow to read about it in the news if you had tried to get out of the car."

Continuing to look at us, the officer said, "You're fortunate that your driver had good sense."

The officer took down all of Liam's information and who all of us were, then they directed us to return home.

As Liam started the car and drove the half-mile back home, none of us even gave a second thought to the fact that the car had no problems.

Addy, Skye, and I felt in a bit of a stupor when we reached Skye's home. We thanked Liam for picking us up, and as we ran to the door, he yelled at us, "You still will need to clean my windows."

Skye replied, "Tomorrow when it's not raining." Then we headed off up to the Turret room. We were all in 'a strange sort of shock.' We didn't say anything. Upon reaching the doorway, we swung it open, and all three of us just climbed onto our beds and gave ourselves time to clear our minds.

We tried to rest while we went over the terrifying events that just happened. Still, our thoughts finally and almost at the same time focused on the discovery at the library.

Addy was the first to sit up and state, "Hey—what happened in the thunderstorm—I really mean 'Happened,' and we are all safe! Don't you both think that it's a bit incredible? So, let's put that behind us and think about what's AHEAD of us!"

Sparked enthusiastically by Addy's remark, I added, "You're definitely right. We know Mr. Callendish died—right above us in that attic! I think, (jumping down from my bunk and placing myself in front of Skye's bunk) that your parents know more than what they are saying. So, don't you think it's time to find out?"

It would be another couple of hours before both Mr. and Mrs. Finnegan would be home from work. So, rather than spend our time in the turret room (which was not particularly where we wanted to be), we decided to make dinner. We hoped to put the Finnegan's in an excellent mood (to answer our questions—of course).

Skye (who was a rather good cook) began making her mother's special meatloaf. I created a nice salad with lettuce, tomatoes, carrots, a few bits of onions, and a tasty lemon poppy seed dressing. Thank goodness they had all the ingredients.

Addy made her favorite dessert 'Marble Brownies.' They were kind of like a half vanilla brownie and the other half with chocolate added, then lightly swirled in the baking pan. Then she prepared a dark chocolate glaze to spoon over them after they cooled from the oven for about fifteen minutes.

Just to make sure we had enough, Skye threw some corn in the microwave to be ready for when her parents arrived.

Skye, Addy, and I set the table and got everything cooked, done, and ready for when the Finnegan's arrived home from work.

Liam—smelling the enticing aroma, woke up from his nap and came downstairs, just as his parents walked through the door.

Skye's parents were pleasantly surprised by the dinner we had just finished laying out on the table. Mrs. Finnegan gave Skye a look of 'wondering what this was all for' but didn't ask at that time. She graciously thanked us, and Mr. Finnegan smiled, gave her a pat on the back, then sat down and started devouring the food we had prepared.

Suspiciously, Mr. Finnegan asked Liam, "What are you doing here? I thought you were spending the whole week with your friend."

Liam replied lazily, "Frankie had an appointment, so he would be gone for 3 to 4 hours, so I came back home."

Skye added, "It's a good thing he did because we needed a ride home from the library, and there was an awful storm, and Liam helped us out."

Mrs. Finnegan replied, "Is that right?"

We sensed that her attitude was more disbelief than thankfulness. Liam wasn't usually a 'helpful lad.'

Meanwhile, Mrs. Finnegan helped herself to small portions and glanced at Skye repeatedly during dinner.

After finishing with Addy's delightful dessert, Skye told her Mom, "We're going to clean up and do the dishes—to thank you for letting us have this week together."

Mrs. Finnegan said pleasingly in her beautiful Irish brogue, "This has been a real treat for us. I want to thank all three of you. BUT, when you've finished, I'd like all of you to come to see Dad and me. OK?"

Glancing at one another nervously, Skye answered, "We'll be up as soon as the dishes are done."

Little did Mrs. Finnegan know that that was exactly what we wanted!

After we finished cleaning up and doing the dishes, we went straight to the living room where Mr. and Mrs. Finnegan were reading and faced them together.

Before Skye's parents got to say a word, Skye asked seriously, "What aren't you telling us about what happened in the attic of the turret room? We've been to the library and read about the 'supposed' murder that took place there. We want to know what YOU know about what happened and why you won't let us go up there?"

Quickly continuing, Skye stated, "You've created a beautiful room in the Turret. And you've let my friends and I sleep there, so I WANT TO KNOW what happened and WHY you would let us stay there! After what we've learned and have been frightened by, I think you owe all of us an explanation!" Tears threatened to fall from Skye's eyes while the three of us stood waiting for their reply.

Chapter 11
Blood in the Attic

Mr. and Mrs. Finnegan looked at one another for quite a while. Then, Mr. Finnegan said to Skye, "I'd like you and your friends to go to your room Skye and stay there until your Mother and I come up to talk to you.

The expression on his face gave us no other option but to do as he said.

Sullenly we walked up to Skye's bedroom and softly plunked down on her bed after closing the door. None of us spoke for several minutes. Finally, Skye said assuredly, "I'm sure they'll be up here soon and let us know what's going on."

I asked Skye, "Do you think THEY really know what's going on?"

Skye gave me a scathing look.

Immediately I said, "I didn't mean that in a bad or stupid way. It's just that they haven't heard the sounds we have or know what we've found out at the library. And they probably think we're just kids, imagining things—which we didn't. Right?"

Addy nodded in agreement, and Skye's anger dissolved.

With her head hanging a bit low, Skye replied, "I'm just afraid they won't understand, and think we are all crazy—which I KNOW we definitely are not!"

After a slight pause, she continued, "I'm worried that they'll come up here and blame it on our imagination and age. I DON'T want the best friends I've ever had OR will ever have being treated like that!"

Addy and I were at a loss for words, so it took me a few minutes to say to Skye, "We ARE your best friends, and NOTHING will change that. So, let's just hear them out—for good or bad—and then the three of us, plus Mr. Grimly and Jeffrey, will decide what to do next. OK?"

I glanced at Addy—who said as cheerfully as possible, "Leira's right. The three of us are like the musketeers, 'One for all and all for one!" Then looking over at Skye, Addy saw her expression go from humiliation to gratitude.

Addy and I smiled happily.

Looking at Addy and I, Skye breathed a sigh of relief, then smirked, asking, "Why was I even worried?"

Addy replied teasingly, "Because you're a goofball sometimes."

Skye scowled, then burst out laughing, and Addy and I joined in. It felt great to let out the laughter. But during our outburst, Mr. and Mrs. Finnegan walked into the room. Our laughter ceased immediately.

The three of us gave our full attention to the Finnegan's as they entered the room. They hadn't given us any time to prepare for their entrance as they gave two short knocks, then opened the door.

We were all sitting on Skye's bed, as Mrs. Finnegan began. "Just stay where you are. Mr. Finnegan and I are going to tell you about some history of this house."

Mrs. Finnegan continued—directing her gaze at Skye, "Something happened in the Attic of the Turret room that we didn't want you to know—or worry about."

Addy, Skye, and I waited breathlessly for Mrs. Finnegan to continue. Finally, after summoning up the courage, she continued, "The last owner of this house committed suicide or was murdered, and it happened in the attic of—the Turret room."

Stunned, anxious, and shocked, Skye, Addy, and I were speechless. Quickly, we tried to keep our horror hidden as we absorbed Mrs. Finnegan's information.

Several seconds flew by before Skye burst out, "What did you just say?"

Mr. Finnegan stepped forward and confronted Skye.

He replied sternly to Skye, "There is NOTHING here to be afraid of. The poor man took his own life—with a knife. That's exactly the reason why the house was sold for a lot less than it is worth!"

Mr. Finnegan continued, "There are no such things as ghosts, and we have a beautiful home in a wonderful neighborhood. That's what you should be thinking of."

Skye asked harshly, "Then why don't you want us to go up into the attic of the Turret?"

Mr. and Mrs. Finnegan backed slowly away, speaking softly to one another.

Returning to face us, Mrs. Finnegan stated quietly, "We didn't want you to see the blood. We were going to have someone come and replace the floorboards before we let you up there." After a slight pause, she continued, "The carpenters are coming next week to replace those parts of the floorboards. We were hoping it would be all done before you or Liam found out. We just didn't want to worry you."

Skye took a step forward towards her parents and stated firmly, "I want to see the attic and the blood and anything else up there—AND—I want my friends there with me!"

The Finnegan's—who were standing a ways back from us whispered to one another for a few minutes. Then, turning back towards us, Mrs. Finnegan replied, "Alright—much to my better judgment, we'll take you up into the attic. BUT we want you to remember that there are no ghosts or anything else macabre there. It's just a horribly sad story of a decent man who lived here."

"Understood?" Mrs. Finnegan asked briskly.

Skye replied immediately, "Yes! All we want is to understand what happened, Skye gulped, and continued, "And—see the evidence. Then we can help put this poor person's life to rest. At least my friends and I won't be frightened to stay in that beautiful room again. Can we go check it out now?"

Mr. and Mrs. Finnegan glanced at one another, then Mr. Finnegan replied, "Alright, let's go up into the attic. You can see for yourselves what your mother and I didn't want you to see OR know about. BUT—I don't want to hear one more word of noises, ghosts, or anything else like that OR the consequences will not be to your liking!" he stated in a stern Irish brogue.

Turning about, with Mrs. Finnegan following, Skye looked back at Addy and me with a bit of nervousness. We followed the Finnegan's up to the 'guest' room and went inside.

Then Skye's father climbed on top of the bed below the attic entrance. He opened the large hatchway and pulled the short ladder down to ascend into the attic.

After he disappeared into the dark, eerie void, Mrs. Finnegan followed him with a bright flashlight. But, as Skye tentatively followed behind, she could see that the entire attic was suddenly full of light!

Quickly glancing down at me, she tried to say light-heartedly, "I guess they found the light switch."

Recognizing her reluctance, I replied shakily, "Well, better real lights than just flashlights!"

Skye replied, "You're right. So—let's get this over with."

She was waiting at the top step for me, thinking I'd be two steps behind. So, I started climbing, and then glanced back at Addy and noticed she was still kneeling on the bed and hadn't taken hold of the ladder.

I gave her a scathing look while saying in an encouraging voice, "Come on, Addy—you don't want to be left here all alone. Do you?"

Addy, glancing behind herself, hustled to step onto the ladder. Skye had already disappeared into the attic, and I followed quickly, with Addy on my heals.

Finally, after the three of us stood together behind Mr. and Mrs. Finnegan, we looked around the attic and took in the beauty of it. It was meant for an artist—with skylights and lots of openness. It couldn't even be imagined from the outside.

I loved art—any kind of art—that's what I wanted to be when I grew up—an Artist! I couldn't help thinking that this would be a dream studio for someone like me.

Abruptly, I noticed the look of 'wonder—curiosity—anger?' that Skye was giving me, and I shifted my focus to the Finnegan's.

They were standing directly under the peak of the turret, and as we approached. Mr. Finnegan held up his hand to stop us from moving forward.

He looked precisely at the three of us at a standstill, then pointed to the floor beneath him.

I redirected my gaze to where he was pointing and saw brownish-red stains on the beautiful maple hardwood floor. It was abruptly clear what I was looking at—the bloodstains of Mr. Callendish!

Mrs. Finnegan realized the emotions we must be going through. She quickly said, "Come downstairs now, and we'll have a nice cup of cocoa and some yummy Scottish shortbread."

After we all climbed the ladder down into the Turret room and proceeded to make our way to the first-floor kitchen, I asked Mrs. Finnegan, "You made 'Scottish shortbread'?"

I added somewhat in a daze, "But you're Irish."

Mrs. Finnegan laughed with a sweet Irish lilt and replied, "Your mum gave me the recipe, and I cannot go a week without making it!"

I smiled, and the tension of my body relaxed. I felt safe again.

After we all had settled in around the kitchen table, Mr. Finnegan started explaining about the death of Mr. Callendish. It wasn't pleasant to hear.

Chapter 12

More Research

It was late, and after all that I had just experienced with my best friends, it was hard to let my body relax after seeing the blood in the Turret attic. A cup of cocoa was good after making a snowman, but… this was completely different.

As Mr. & Mrs. Finnegan, Skye, Addy, and I sat around the kitchen table, they began to tell us what little they knew.

Mr. Finnegan started, often pausing, "You girls need to understand a few things that we knew about before we bought the house."

"We knew that Mr. Callendish had taken his life in the attic of the turret room. We also knew that he used the attic for an artist studio. He was an extremely gifted painter. His art was his joy—as was his wife."

Mr. Finnegan continued, "Mr. Callendish was a very wealthy man. His art was a hobby, but he made his fortune on 'Callendish Candies.'"

Interrupting, I asked, "Callendish Candies? I've never heard of them."

Mr. Finnegan replied, "Well, I don't doubt that you would have. They stopped producing them shortly before his death."

Addy asked quickly, "If the candies were so good, then why did they stop making them?"

Mr. Finnegan replied, "I have no idea. They were not sold where we lived. So, we didn't know anything about them or Mr. Callendish when we bought the property. It wasn't until we lived here a while that we discovered some additional information about why the home was listed at a price lower than it was worth. Of course, the realtor had to disclose the fact that the previous owner had died here."

Mr. Finnegan stated in conclusion while looking at Skye, "This home is everything that we wanted for our family. Mr. Callendish's demise was a dreadful occurrence, but it has no bearing on 'OUR' lives here. There are NO GHOSTS or any other strange happenings that cannot be explained, AND I'd like to move on with our new lives and new friends—wouldn't you?"

Skye, whose gaze her father was mostly directed at, glanced at Addy and me. Both of us gave her encouraging nods. Finally, she replied to her father, "Dad, I'm glad that you've told us what you know, AND that you've shown us what really happened to Mr. Callendish—kind of if you know what I mean. And, now that we know, I think our imaginations won't 'see' what's not there."

"But, if you and Mom don't mind, I'd like to do some more research at the library, with Addy and Leira to understand better why this happened."

Skye looked at Addy and me for agreement, and we both gave her nods of approval.

Skye's Mom replied, "I think that would be a positive thing to do. Obviously, your father and I would be interested in your findings. Still, you could also use your research for school projects—like the one you are doing on our town history."

Mrs. Finnegan continued, "This idea you have is brilliant! It will help put to rest your anxiety living here and possibly be rewarded at school. All three of you will benefit from the research."

Mrs. Finnegan concluded, "I'm very proud of you for taking this path to conquer your fears—and don't forget—you have other friends willing to help you."

Glancing at Addy, then at Skye and myself, Mrs. Finnegan concluded, "Mr. Grimly and Jeffrey. Now off to bed with the lot of you!"

We walked sleepily up to Skye's bedroom, where we spent the rest of the night—what was left of it.

Mrs. Finnegan never woke us up, and it was me who woke up first after ten o'clock in the morning. Groggily, I got up and gently shook Skye awake. She woke fairly quickly, still a bit disturbed by the events of the past twelve hours.

Ghost in the Turret

After rubbing the sleep from her eyes, she asked me, "Do you want to wake up, Addy?"

I replied, "No, let's do it together."

Skye frowned and replied dismally, "OK."

Reluctantly, both having the same idea, we ran over to Addy's bed, pounced on it, and I yelled teasingly, "GET up, you LAZY RAGGED DRESSED TINKER!" We need your help to do our investigation!"

Addy was—terrified, angry, perplexed, and surprised—before she could fully understand what was happening. But, instead of being mad at us—she baffled us by grabbing Skye and me into a great big bear hug and exclaimed, "All for one and one for all!"

Skye and I were shocked into silence by Addy quoting 'The Three Musketeers', but then again, that's what we thought we were—in our own little way.

So—with the three of us smiling, we went downstairs to breakfast, then cleaned up, and Mrs. Finnegan drove us to the Public Library to continue our research.

After arriving, I said to Addy and Skye, "We won't have a lot of time, so let's divvy up the research."

Addy replied, "What do you have in mind?"

I said, "Well, one of us could check the internet for any information on Mr. Callendish's death. And one of us could research the old newspapers printed at that time… and that would leave….?"

Skye pounced on that question replying triumphantly, "Investigating what happened to MRS. Callendish!"

The three of us were stunned by Skye's idea! Looking at Skye with some concern, I asked, "Do you realize what you've just said?"

Addy waited for Skye's answer breathlessly.

Skye finally replied quietly, but seriously, "Yes. I think there may be a possibility that Mr. Callendish didn't commit suicide!"

Giving my head a quick shake—as though to wake myself up, I answered, "Well, OK then, let's get busy doing our research before we have to go home—or we won't have accomplished anything. We have four hours, so let's meet at the research table next to the back entrance. Agreed?"

Skye replied with a nod of her head, and Addy said, "I'll be there."

We set off on our different tasks to try and combine the results to one conclusion.

At the appointed time, the three of us gathered cautiously at the prearranged area. It was obvious that all three of us had uncovered more information.

We settled down with copies of newspaper articles, website downloads, and even magazines. Looking at all we had gathered, we realized this would be much more complicated than we thought. And maybe even more dangerous than any of us—or even our families might know.

I started first with what I was able to find on the internet about Skye's home and what happened to Mr. Callendish.

Taking a deep breath, I began, "The internet was less useful than I thought it would be. There was a story of Mr. Callendish's suicide and how tragic it was for a 60-year-old man who developed wonderful sorts of candy could do something so horrible."

To me, the story was kind of odd because it didn't show any respect for what he had accomplished. It pretty much gave a bad name to Callendish Candies, which could have led to it being partly discontinued." I found very few internet sites about it. This particular one I found was upsetting and undeserving of his accomplishments! None of the articles I found mentioned that it could have been murder. That's all I could find out now on the internet."

"What about you, Addy? Did you find anything in the local newspapers?"

Addy replied, "Well, a bit more than you did, Leira—which kind of surprises me. I thought the internet knew tons more than any town newspaper! That's definitely something to keep in mind when writing our next school report!"

With a smirk (that Skye and I didn't fully appreciate at the time), she continued, "There were three articles written at the time of his death. The first—of course, was written by his widow, Evelyn Renee Coleman Callendish. I have a copy here, but basically, it's a sickening, overdone eulogy—if you know what I mean."

Skye interrupted, "No. I really don't know what you mean. What's a 'eulogy'?"

Addy explained patiently, "A eulogy is usually a speech someone gives in honor of a person who has died at their funeral."

Addy continued, "In this article, they quote her eulogy."

Addy passed us a copy of the newspaper article. It read:

"With tears flowing abundantly, Mrs. Callendish stood upright, trembling in front of her beloved husbands' coffin. She delivered an extremely moving eulogy in honor of her husband while bravely facing family, friends, and bystanders. This is a quote from that moment."

> *"My dearest family and friends, I am inconsolable in my grief about my husband's death and the manner of it. Regrettably, I feel responsible for such a hideous end to his brilliant life. If I had only known the depth of his despair, I think I could have prevented it.*
>
> *Callendish Candies—of which he took such pride—has been closed, and as for me—I am selling our home and moving elsewhere to try and start my life over again.*
>
> *Thank you all for your kind words of sympathy, but in order to get beyond this, I need to move on."*

"This reporter cannot believe how strong a person Mrs. Callendish was while delivering this emotional speech. I'm sure the community will wish her all the best, as do I."

Brianna Scarborough—Reporter for the Daily Herald.

After reading the newspaper article, I looked worriedly at Skye as Addy also did. I asked Skye, "What did you find out about what happened to Mrs. Callendish?" Skye grinned like a cat that caught a mouse… as she began to tell us things we couldn't quite believe!"

Skye began, "Well, first of all, Mrs. Callendish had her husband cremated as the coroner had ruled it a suicide. And, after checking the records here—she collected $1,000,000!"

Addy interrupted, "I thought you couldn't collect life insurance if you committed suicide!"

Skye raising a brow, replied, "Not if there is a special clause in the document—which he had!"

I asked briskly, "And how do YOU know all about this 'Special Clause'?

Skye replied, "My uncle Shamus is a lawyer who specializes in this stuff."

"I thought once I found out about the inheritance that I should write to him. He even sent me the documentation related to what happed here and highlighted the important parts." Skye grinned while continuing, "I think he's almost as interested as we are!"

I was quiet for a while as I absorbed the information I had just learned.

Addy asked after a few minutes, "What's going on, Leira? What are you thinking?"

With my face draining of color, I replied very seriously, "I'm getting the feeling that it wasn't suicide—but a MURDER!"

Chapter 13
Notes And Phone Calls

My friends, Skye and Addy, stared at me in disbelief. I thought I could hear their hearts hammering, but truthfully, I think it was mine.

Addy stammered, "A MURDER—for real?"

I looked back and forth between Addy and Skye and asked, "Doesn't it make sense? I mean—from what we've already learned, Mr. Callendish was incredibly happy. He had an awesome candy business, but all the time he wanted to do what he really loved—which was painting."

I continued, "He had a beautiful wife he loved very much. And there was nothing ever written about him that we could find about being anything but grateful and happy with his life."

"So why would a successful, happy man commit suicide?"

Skye replied, "I think before we go any further that we need to do a LOT more investigating. And—I'm sure Mr. Grimly knows more than he's already told us."

Addy agreed wholeheartedly, "Yeah—he definitely seemed a bit nervous when we've talked to him about it! So, I say, we grab Fluffums, Shugar, and Katie and visit Mr. Grimly! What do you think, Leira?"

I replied, "Let's go!"

Of course, Skye and Addy each had to 'explain' to their parents that we had promised to take our puppies over to Mr. Grimly so he could visit with all of us. And, so Puffin could unite with her babies (although—I don't think Puffin really understood that they WERE her babies, but she enjoyed romping around with them anyway.

We led the pups down the street towards Grimly Manor. Addy noticed that Jeffrey was looking out his picture window as we walked by.

Addy commented, "I know he's been trying to help us, but he still gives me the creeps sometimes."

Skye replied, "Don't worry, Addy, he won't bother you unless he knows you're OK with it. I made sure to tell my brother Liam to keep an eye on him."

Skye grinned proudly for making sure her friends were safe.

Addy and I both noticed but didn't respond. I don't think either of us had much faith in Liam's protection after all he had done to Skye. But Addy and I didn't say anything, just gave each other a 'knowing' look.

We arrived at Mr. Grimly's decrepit mansion unannounced because he didn't have a phone. Then, we proceeded to knock loudly on the door. We could hear Puffin barking up a storm, anxious to see who was there. Our three growing pups began barking and howling incessantly to play with their Mom.

After about three to four minutes of howling and barking, we were reaching the end of our patience.

Skye started seriously banging on the new maple front door.

Addy finally stopped her, exclaiming, "Hey! Not so hard, or you'll put your fist through it. You're lucky Leira's Dad replaced the old one, you know."

Skye stopped, turned, and asked Addy and me, "Well, what DO you want me to do?"

Skye continued to angrily question us, "What if he's in there hurt or worse? I think he would have come to the door by now—don't you?"

The three of us continued arguing as the dogs kept barking in a frenzy. A few more minutes ticked by, and finally—the front door slowly creaked open.

Mr. Grimly stood there with tears welling up in his eyes and said shakily, "Come in."

Immediately our demeanor changed from anger to concern for our good friend. I supposed none of us wanted or knew what to say next.

All our pups were happily playing with their Mom and left the room seeking treats they knew were hidden there and went to find them.

Mr. Grimly slumped down into his favorite comfy chair in a way that 'said' to me 'defeat.'

Addy, Skye, and I sat in our usual places on the musty old sofa.

Mr. Grimly sniffled a few times, then wiped the trickle of a few tears from underneath his new healing eyelids. We noticed how careful he was not to aggravate his recent reconstructive surgery.

We waited patiently for him to speak, but I couldn't help but speak up first as minutes ticked by. I asked him softly, "What is it, Mr. Grimly?" I paused, then proceeded, "Whatever it is—all three of us want to help—no matter what it is."

Pleadingly, after several moments went by, I said, "You're our best friend, and you can count on us to help you. I know we're young… but…"

My sentence drifted off because I didn't know how to convince him to trust us—but Skye did!

Immediately, Skye continued my sentence, "Yeah—we are young, but we're also BRAVE, STUBBORN, and FEARLESS—well at times. Most of all, we've come through those terrifying experiences BECAUSE of our friendship and trust in one another! So—YOU need to believe in us now and let us help you."

Addy finally spoke up by asking, "Well? Are we your friends or not?"

Mr. Grimly slowly raised his eyes to the three of us as his tears slowly stopped. He took a deep breath to keep his emotions in control. He finally began by saying, "All three of you are so bright, compassionate and inquisitive—sometimes more than you should be."

"I know why you have come just now, and I think I can guess what you are going to ask, which is why my heart is heavy."

I asked, after a slight pause, "Why would your heart be heavy if all we want to do is understand what happened to Mr. Callendish? Why does that upset you?"

Skye and Addy listened carefully, waiting for his answer.

Mr. Grimly took another deep breath. Then replied, "Because—I think there is a possibility that if you continue to investigate his death—that it could possibly put you in danger."

The three of us gasped, but Mr. Grimly sternly restated "POSSIBLY." I don't know everything that happened to that poor man or why he would have taken his life. Still, something tells me that it's not something that you should concern yourselves with or poke your noses into any further than you have! Do you understand what I'm saying?"

Addy replied, "I think you're worried that IF Mr. Callendish's 'suicide' wasn't a suicide, then by doing more research, it might put us in danger. Is that it?"

Skye and I looked at Addy, then over to Mr. Grimly and waited tensely for him to answer.

Mr. Grimly kept us waiting a long time before he said, "A tragedy has already occurred—there should never be another."

He continued, "I can't say anymore right now, but—please promise me that you won't go searching for more clues."

Skye, Addy, and I looked uncomfortably at one another. With the most honest answer I could give him, I replied.

"We promise not to search for any more clues, BUT—we can't promise the clues won't come to us."

Nodding his head, Mr. Grimly answered (with a tiny smirk), "I understand what you're saying, and so I need to ask one more thing. IF the clues come to you—will you tell me and let me help you?"

Skye pounced on his question with an enthusiastic, "Yes—of course! I can't believe you even had to ask us that."

Mr. Grimly looked at Skye and replied, "I will always trust the three of you, Skye, but I just needed to reassure myself that you will include me and let me help you."

He continued, "At my age, I've been through a lot and have seen a lot, and I just want to be sure that I'm there if you need me. Do you understand?"

He looked at Addy and me after speaking to Skye. We all nodded our heads, and I said, "Don't worry, Mr. Grimly—if a pin drops—we'll tell you." Then smiling, I continued, "Unless, of course, it's my mother dropping one while working on her stitchery!"

Mr. Grimly relaxed and said, "Well, you all better get on home and get your chores done and take care of these pups—they won't be pups much longer."

He arose from his favorite chair and walked us to the front door. As we walked down his driveway towards home, I glanced back as he slowly closed the new door and noticed the worried look on his face.

We dropped off our pups at home (after refreshing the water and giving them their meal), then headed back to Skye's house.

Skye enthusiastically said, "Mail's here!"

I asked her, "Why are you so excited about the mail? I never get anything."

Skye blushed a bit, and so did Addy.

I immediately asked, "Hey! What's going on that I don't know about? SPEAK—or else!"

"Else, what?" Skye asked.

I stammered, "Well… I don't know. I heard it in a movie, and I thought it would get you to tell me what I think you are BOTH hiding from me."

Addy's eyes glanced downwards. Skye hesitantly replied, "Well, I've been checking the mail every day to see if I got a note or something from your cousin Luke in Arizona."

Abruptly, before I could ask anything more, Skye added, smiling, "And Addy has been checking her mail every day for a letter. You know, from Rob—that Indian guy in Arizona."

Addy burst out, "Hey! Don't call him that—he's not just 'That Indian Guy,' He's my friend! We wouldn't be here if it wasn't for him… well, mostly."

I burst out in a slight fit of hysterical laughter, thinking of my two best friends looking for 'love notes,' but I suddenly stopped when I saw the severe and angry looks on their faces.

"So.", I asked Skye, "Did you get anything in the mail?"

Addy and I waited as Skye flipped through the stack in her hand. Smiling, she said, "Here's one for me!"

Expectantly, we waited for the details.

Her cheery face turned to a perplexed look as she looked at the front and then the back of the envelope.

I asked, "Well, who is it from?"

She replied, "I don't know yet. There's no return address, AND there's not even a stamp."

Addy tried to hurry her along, saying, "Well, open it silly and tell us what it says."

Just then, from inside the house, we heard the phone ringing. Skye, as distracted as she was, said, "I need to answer that."

She quickly unlocked the door and raced to the phone. We were right behind her as she answered, "Hello?"

After a moment, she asked, "Is there someone there?"

Her face turned ashen as she listened to the caller and then, after a few moments, slowly hung up the phone as if in a trance.

Worriedly, I quickly demanded, "Who was that? What did they say?"

Addy looked on in concern as Skye replied, slightly dazed, "I don't know who it was. The voice was muffled, but they said, "You had better read your mail quickly if you want to live…"

Skye grabbed the letter she had previously found addressed to her and began to rip it open in fear.

I slapped my hand over the letter. And as Skye looked at me in rage and desperation, I said quietly but firmly, "This is NOT a time to panic, it's time to figure out what is going on in a very, calm and smart way."

I continued, "So, let's take a couple of deep breaths, sit down on the sofa, and you can slowly read the letter aloud. Then, we can decide what to do next. Agreed?"

Addy immediately replied, "Leira's right. We just can't jump to any hasty conclusions."

Pointedly Addy asked Skye, "Are you calm enough to do what Leira suggested?"

Silence filled the room, and Skye stared blankly ahead, but suddenly it seemed like a light turned on for her. She replied after exhaling a deep breath, "I'm OK now, and yes, let's sit down and read the note together, and ALL three of us will decide what to do next."

Chapter 14

Cherry-O-Cream Pie and Mrs. Finnegan

Skye proceeded to finish opening the letter, but much more carefully and slowly.

Addy jumped up and raised her hands at lightning speed with a 'STOP' motion and yelled, "WAIT!"

Skye and I snapped our heads around in fear, and I almost leaped out of the chair, shouting, "WHAT is it?"

Addy, a bit on edge, answered, "We—don't know what is in that envelope, or who it was who called. So, just to be safe, I think we should put some kind of gloves on before touching it anymore."

Skye said, confused and a bit sarcastically, "I don't know what you are talking about or why we need gloves. Have you been eating too many cookies and candies?"

Addy huffed in exasperation and replied, "NO! Don't you understand? This could be evidence, and we don't want to muck it up with any more of our fingerprints."

I could sense Skye was ready to tangle with Addy, so I spoke up abruptly, "Skye! Addy could be right. We don't know 'yet' what is in that letter. And the person on the phone definitely seemed to be threatening us or YOU."

I continued, "Even if it seems silly right now, I agree with Addy. We shouldn't contaminate the letter any more than it has been already—agreed?"

73

Skye rolled her eyes and replied, "Agreed—I'll go get some rubber gloves from the kitchen."

As Skye left, Addy asked me, "Do you think I'm nuts or what?"

I replied, "Addy, it was a good idea. We don't know what we've gotten ourselves into, and it's better to be safe than sorry."

Addy relaxed a bit afterward, and Skye was back in a couple of minutes with two sets of rubber gloves. She looked at us and said, "Sorry. I could only find these two sets, and one has been used for a week or so."

I commented, "I think we should use the ones from the package that haven't been opened yet."

Addy nodded her head in agreement, and Skye carefully opened the package. Without touching the outside of the gloves, she placed her hands inside them. Then—she carefully removed the letter, holding it by the edges, and started to read.

> *I am DEAD now that you are reading this—I took my own life because I could not bear another moment of my artistic failure. My Candy factory made me wealthy and took care of those I loved. But I HATED candy—it was self-indulgence for those who never knew poverty and hunger.*
>
> *My art was my salvation and triumph, but no one ever saw that—they only saw the candy and the sweetness. It wasn't sweet—it was poison—my ART was the sweetness to be inhaled by a glance.*
>
> *No one ever understood it, so I can rise to the heavens with MY sweetness—my art by leaving now.*

"Whoa!" Skye uttered, taking a step back. "So, he did take his own life, and here for some time, we've thought he was murdered."

I spoke slightly with anger, "I DON'T believe any of this! I don't believe in ghosts! I don't think a ghost called you on the phone. I find it particularly unbelievable that a few moments after receiving THE letter in the mail, the phone rings. And someone is telling you to read the letter, and it turns out to be a suicide note!"

Skye and Addy were both stunned by my single outburst.

I took a deep breath to collect my thoughts, then I continued with fiery determination, "This was NO suicide, and WE will find out the truth! Are you with me or not?"

Even Skye looked a bit taken aback by the tone of my words, but meekly (for her), she replied, "Of course I'm with you. I'm just not sure what the next step is."

Addy, who was still a bit startled, said, "Yes, we are both with you. But, I'd like to make sure we plan this together and also have someone 'older' to rely on for guidance."

All three of us looked at one another—smiled, and in unison said, "Mr. Grimly!"

We had decided before we showed Mr. or Mrs. Finnegan the note that we should see Mr. Grimly to see what he thought of it.

Skye stated, "If my Mom or Dad knew of this, they wouldn't let us sleep in the Turret room. So, I think seeing Mr. Grimly first and getting his advice would be best."

Addy looked at Skye in shock and asked in astonishment, "You WANT to spend the night in the Turret room? Are you insane?"

Skye replied crisply, "How the heck else are we supposed to solve this? There are NO ghosts! WE—the three of us—possibly with the help of one or two other friends are going to get to the bottom of this—even if my Mom has to sleep upstairs with us!"

I cooed sarcastically at Addy, "Or Jeffrey?"

As Addy started to scowl, I interrupted, then apologized, and stated, "The most important thing right now is to go see Mr. Grimly. So—let's quit our stupid bickering and go visit him."

After receiving permission to visit Mr. Grimly under the ruse of taking the pups over to see Puffin again, we set off. Cautiously we approached the door because we didn't really know if he was sleeping or 'whatever.'

Skye repeatedly rapped on the door, and we were happy to hear Puffin barking loudly on the other side. All three of our pups tugged at us, barking and howling to visit their Mom.

Soon, we heard the muffled voice of Mr. Grimly telling Puffin to hush, and then the door slowly opened.

Mr. Grimly looked sad—or something—I couldn't find the right word in my head.

He finally said, "Come in."

All three of us entered with our pups going off to play or terrorize their Mom, while we sat down on his tattered, old sofa.

He looked at the three of us and, with a deep breath, asked, "Did a clue find you?"

I replied firmly, "Yes."

Then, I handed him the letter that Skye had received in the mail.

Mr. Grimly read the letter carefully, then replied, "I think you are all clever enough to know that Mr. Callendish didn't write this."

Mr. Grimly continued, "He's dead and buried and has been for a long time, and I believe if this letter could be analyzed, that you would find it wasn't written before his death."

The three of us listened, amazed, and bewildered a bit.

Chewing on my lower lip while thinking, I finally asked, "How would you know that?"

Mr. Grimly answered with a question, "Are you spending the night in the Turret room tonight?"

We all nodded while stating firmly, "Yes."

Mr. Grimly said at last, "I need to get some rest right now. But, make sure there is an adult with you tonight in the room—AND—if you are to solve this—spend the WHOLE night. If an adult won't stay the whole time, then… he looked at us sheepishly and then showed us a disposable cell phone. Written on a piece of paper was the number. He handed it to Skye and said, "Call me, and I'll come right over."

We were all so dumbfounded that we couldn't say a word. Skye reached out her hand and took the piece of paper, then we called our pups and left the manor.

With our puppies in tow, the three of us walked with determination down the road to our homes. We were silent while considering what Mr. Grimly had said.

Ghost in the Turret

Just as Addy was about to speak up—I interrupted, holding a finger to my lips, I gathered Skye and Addy around me.

With resolve, I told Skye, "We have to spend the night in the Turret room, AND your Mom needs to be there! That's what Mr. Grimly was telling us—that we need to have at least one of your parents believe us, and I think your Mom will."

Glancing nervously between Skye and Addy, I waited for their answer.

It came quickly. Skye replied, "She'll sleep up there with us tonight, or I am not Skye Finnegan!"

Addy and I responded with thankful smiles.

I told Skye, "I'll be back over after taking care of my pets, and I'll even bring over a pie for dinner. It'll be a sneaky surprise to butter up your parents."

Addy asked, "What kind of pie?"

I replied, "One of my favorites—Cherry-O Cream Pie! Everyone will love it."

I arrived back at Skye's home to spend the evening. Mrs. Finnegan had prepared a basic but truly remarkable Macaroni and Cheese casserole with salad and broccoli. Of course, the highlight of the fantastic delicious dinner was the dessert I had brought.

Everyone thoroughly enjoyed the pie I'd made.

Mrs. Finnegan was not very enthusiastic about spending the night in the turret room. Still, Skye, along with Addy and I wanted her to realize (without telling her) that something very REAL and SCARY was going on. The three of us were afraid, but we felt more protected with Mrs. Finnegan in the room with us. At least if something happened, an adult would be there to back us up and protect us. Also, Mr. Finnegan was right downstairs if we needed him.

Even though Skye's Mom wasn't too excited about spending the night with us, what really intrigued us was 'why' she wasn't. It seemed like most parents would love to spend the night 'overhearing' the conversation of her daughter and friends. But she wasn't.

It was just the opposite—she seemed almost frightened about staying with us in the Turret room. She left for a little while, and I asked Skye, "Why is your Mom afraid of staying with us?"

Addy interrupted, "Yeah. Maybe we shouldn't stay here tonight. I mean—if your Mom is scared, then I think we shouldn't stay here."

Skye scoffed at our being cowards and replied, "She's not scared. She just doesn't want to deal with three jumpy fraidy-cats who will probably keep her up all night. There's nothing to worry about. My Dad is downstairs, and we just need her here in case."

I asked seriously, "In case of what?"

Skye answered, "In case Jeffrey or a ghost pop in!" Then Skye grinned and let out a bit of a chuckle. "Seriously," she continued, "I don't know what might happen. But I'll feel a lot better with my Mom here. So, let's just get ready for bed, make sure the windows are locked, and watch a boring movie to put us to sleep."

Addy and I agreed and got into our jammies, then crawled into bed. None of us chose the bunk beneath the attic entrance.

When Mrs. Finnegan returned, ready for bed, we had put on a classic old movie we thought she would enjoy but put us to sleep.

She looked at her choices of beds left, and she chose the bottom bunk bed beneath the Turret Attic. The only other one available was the top bunk beneath it…

I wondered if she wished Mr. Finnegan was there above her, but I knew he had to leave incredibly early in the morning for a business flight.

As she settled in and turned toward the TV, she let out a small exhalation of disgust.

Skye immediately asked, "Mom, is there something wrong?"

Mrs. Finnegan replied, "No, it's alright. I'm just not thrilled with your choice of movies."

Skye answered, "Good, we picked it out because it's boring, and all of us just want to fall asleep."

Mrs. Finnegan replied, "Well, why don't you shut off the movie and put on the CD player with soothing music instead?"

Skye replied, "We'll fall asleep quicker with the boring movie."

"Ugh." Mrs. Finnegan replied. Then she threw the blankets over her head and faced the wall while trying to get to sleep—which she did—until she awoke two hours later to the sound of creaking steps from the attic above her!

Chapter 15
Sell the House?

Mrs. Finnegan, suddenly wide-awake, tried desperately not to overreact. Taking several deep breaths and exhaling slowly, she listened carefully. A few minutes passed, and Mrs. Finnegan began to think that her previous thoughts were just a bad dream. Just while starting to relax—she heard it again!

There were definitely creaking sounds coming from straight above her in the attic. Her mind was suddenly filled with different avenues of escape—'Grab the kids and take them downstairs' or 'Rush to her husband and have him investigate' or even crawl up into the attic with a bat and face whatever?

None of the options that were running through her head seemed safe or gutsy enough to go through with. Another few moments passed, and upon hearing more creaking footsteps, she quickly woke the three of us up, corralled us to the steps, and shuffled us downstairs.

All three of us, sleepy, terrified, and confused, blurted out, "What's happened? What's going on?"

I was in front, and as we scrambled down the stairs, I stumbled as everyone behind me was pushing. Luckily, I grabbed hold of the railing while Skye, who was behind me, grabbed the back of my pajamas.

There wasn't any time to thank Skye as Mrs. Finnegan hushed us up quickly by snapping, "Just be quiet! Now!" When we tried to ask questions, she shushed us, then made us wait in the sitting room outside her bedroom, but we all noticed that she locked the door to the hallway before leaving us. We had no idea what conversation was transpiring between Mr. and Mrs. Finnegan, but it lasted for a while.

Trembling, I asked Skye, "Do you have any idea what's going on?"

Skye replied worriedly, "No. I don't have any clue. Did either of you hear anything before my Mom woke us up?"

Addy and I both shook our heads-no.

Skye replied, "I fell asleep so quickly. That movie was totally lame. I was so tired from everything that happened today that I didn't hear anything until my Mom shook me, and even then, it was hard to wake up."

I said thoughtfully, "So, your Mom must have heard something for her to be so scared. Do you think it came from the attic?"

Skye replied, "Duh!"

Angrily I retorted, "Don't make me sound stupid! I'm just trying to figure out what's happening. Maybe we should go back up there and check it out."

Addy stiffened up and burst out, "Are you crazy? There may be a ghost or worse up there! If Mrs. Finnegan was afraid for all of us, then the last thing we should do is go there!"

Skye—not as fearless as usual, agreed. She said, "Let's just wait and see what my parents say."

"Alright." I said, "But if we miss something important, then don't say I was the one who was too scared."

Addy and Skye both looked at me with a bit of anger and humiliation.

Just then, the bedroom door opened, and Mr. and Mrs. Finnegan stepped out. Mr. Finnegan came out first, and I noticed at once that he had a GUN in his hand. He tried to hide it from sight, but because I was all the way to the left of my friends, I saw enough of it.

I didn't dare say anything to my friends, as I was sure that Skye's parents didn't want us to know.

Mr. Finnegan addressed all of us. "Skye, your Mom has told me what she heard in the attic of the Turret room, and I'm going to go look. I'm sure it's just the trees brushing against the house. It's very windy tonight, so it also could just be creaking floorboards from the shoddy construction job of the room and the attic."

Ghost in the Turret

"Either way, I'd like all of you to remain here with your Mom (Mrs. Finnegan) until I come back and make sure everything is fine—which by the way—I'm sure it will be."

"Fiona," Mr. Finnegan said, addressing his wife, "Please keep the children here and if I have any problems—which I don't believe I will—I have my cell, and I'll call 911, then let you know."

At that statement, all three of us pounced on him with jumbled questions as to why he would need to call 911.

Calmly, he replied there would most likely be no need, but it was always better to be prepared.

As Mr. Finnegan walked off down the hallway to the door leading to the Turret room, the three of us (and Mrs. Finnegan) waited nervously for what was to come.

In the sitting room waiting for any peep from upstairs, Skye asked her Mom, "Why did you buy this house if you knew someone died here?"

Addy and I listened patiently for her response. Reluctantly, she replied, "I don't know. All I was thinking of was a new start, in a new place, in a beautiful home, where I could raise my family and give them all the benefits of a good life. I never once thought of asking about the history of the home. It never crossed my mind—it was so beautiful and away from all the disappointing things we left behind."

Skye hesitantly asked, "When did you find out about Mr. Callendish, and what happened?"

Mrs. Finnegan thought carefully before she answered. "Your Dad told me after I had started the restoration of the room for your birthday. I was a might ticked off that he didn't tell me before we bought the house."

"He didn't make much of it, but before we put too much money into making the room really special, he thought I should know. He knew that you didn't know what was going on, and he was giving me a chance to change my mind—I guess."

She continued, "I spent about a week going over the information about what happened, and your father brought me up into the attic."

"The suicide and the blood—upset me, but I truly don't believe in evil spirits or ghosts, or I never would have completed the room—OR—let you stay there!"

Mrs. Finnegan stated firmly, "I believe that whatever is happening is NOT supernatural. Still, regardless, something is happening—most likely a prankster. But your father will get to the bottom of this now that he knows, and we'll do whatever he thinks is best."

Skye asked hesitantly, "What about tonight?"

Mrs. Finnegan replied, "Even if your father doesn't find anything, then I still think it's best for the three of you to stay together in your room Skye. And—if any of you are frightened, then I will be more than happy to take all three of you over to Leira's house to spend the night."

The three of us in unison shook our heads 'No,' and I replied, "We'll be fine in Skye's room."

We waited a while longer before Mr. Finnegan came downstairs.

Expectantly, we looked up at him for his response.

When he gave it—we all felt a bit uneasy.

Mr. Finnegan told us calmly, "I didn't see or hear anything in the attic, and I sat there quite a while. I even embarrassed myself by 'calling out' to 'a presence,' but no answer."

Mr. Finnegan continued, "I don't believe any of you imagined anything. I'm just saying that I didn't see or hear anything. But to be on the safe side and make sure you girls can get some sleep, I suggest you sleep in Skye's room right across from ours."

"Now, if you ladies don't mind, I'd like to get some sleep."

He said, "Good night.", then left with Mrs. Finnegan. The three of us turned towards Skye's bedroom, and after entering, we all stopped short and remembered that we left our sleeping 'buddies' in the turret room.

The three of us looked at each other fearfully, and finally, Skye asked, "We can get up there in back in less than two minutes! AND—we can't leave them to spend the night there alone!"

"On the count of three—let's rescue our sleeping buddies. ONE—TWO—THREE!"

We raced down the hallway, up the stairs, and into the Turret bedroom.

Next, we grabbed our sleeping buddies, ran back downstairs without stumbling, and into Skye's bedroom.

After slamming the door shut, we jumped into her new comfy Queen sized bed. As we snuggled up together with our sleeping buddies held tightly in our hands, we began to relax.

The next morning, when I woke up, I could see that Addy had been awake for some time. We glanced at one another for a minute or so before I finally asked, "Should we wake up Skye?"

Addy shifted her eyes away from me and, with seeming reluctance, replied, "If you want me to. But will you do it? I really didn't sleep much, and I don't know if I could deal with her in a bad mood. Right now—I almost just want to go home."

Hastily, I said, "It's OK. I'll wake Skye up, and then we can go downstairs—have some breakfast and decide what to do next."

Addy suddenly turned her head toward the door and sniffed a few times. Her eyes lit up a bit, and she was about to say…

Skye popped up from her bed just then and exclaimed, "BACON"!

Suddenly, the three of us grabbed our robes, shoved our feet into slippers, and raced down to the kitchen.

Mr. and Mrs. Finnegan had finished cooking, and the plates were already laid out when we arrived!

After all the terrifying things that had happened during the night—our tummy's took control. We almost drooled as a massive bowl of fluffy, steaming scrambled eggs were placed in front of us. Next, an enormous heated plate of bacon, a skillet full of hash brown potatoes, and a triple-decker stack of different types of toasted bread was placed on the table.

There was also butter, three types of jam, and carafes filled with Orange juice, apple juice, grape juice, and icy water. We all chose whatever we wanted.

Our delicious breakfast put our nighttime horror away for a bit (just a little bit). Still, as the hunger and need dissipated, Skye, Addy, and I started glancing at one another, wondering who would bring up last night's 'disturbances.'

It was Skye who finally spoke up when everyone had nearly finished their breakfast. She asked her parents, "So what are we going to do about the strange things going on in the Turret room and the attic?"

Mr. Finnegan looked gravely over at Mrs. Finnegan, and she reached out and took his hand. Then, looking directly at Skye—told her, "We are putting the house up for sale." Your mother and I will not live in a home where our children are terrified."

Skye, Addy, and I gasped. The three of us making a jumbled mess of what we were trying to say. Skye finally shushed us and begged her parents, "I don't want to move! These are the only best friends I've ever had. And I love everything here: The Davie's, The MacGregor's, Mr. Grimly, even begrudgingly Jeffrey. I've never lived in a place where I've felt so at home with such good people."

"Mom—Dad," Please give us some time to figure out what is really going on here before you sell the house—I'm begging you."

I leaned over to Addy and whispered, "It's a good thing we didn't show them the letter or tell them about the phone call, or that would be the end of it."

As a few drops of tears coursed down Skye's face, Mr. and Mrs. Finnegan spoke quietly, and the three of us waited for the answer.

Finally, Mr. Finnegan spoke, "Skye—I understand how much your new friends mean to you. But under the circumstances, your Mother and I feel it's best to put the house up for sale."

Interrupting the sobs that came from the three of us, he continued, "My job is still here, so even though we will be moving—it will be someplace awfully close to here. So, you'll be very near one another, maybe even attending the same school. BUT I don't want to hear another word about the Turret attic and what happened or what you heard or saw. That is FINAL!"

Mr. Finnegan threw his finely embroidered Irish napkin down on the table, gave Mrs. Finnegan an anguished look, and left the room abruptly. All Mrs. Finnegan could do was look at us sympathetically, shake her head slightly, and say to the three of us, "I'm sorry—but I agree with your father. We'll be talking to a realtor tomorrow."

Skye yelled, "Mom—NO!" but Mrs. Finnegan left the table to follow her husband.

After she disappeared, Addy, Skye, and I looked at one another in desperation. Then, Skye said to us with such determination, "Mr.

Grimly said there were "NO GHOSTS"! So—let's prove him right and find out what is REALLY going on."

Skye looked at us slyly with a twinkle in her eyes and waited for our reply.

Addy and I started to grin simultaneously, and I replied, "Let's make a plan—but we'll have to hurry, or your house will be sold!"

Skye replied ominously, "I won't EVER let that happen."

Chapter 16

Murder Or Suicide?

That night we spent in Skye's bedroom—with the door locked. After crawling into our makeshift beds, I asked Skye and Addy, "OK—my brilliant friends, what's the plan?"

Skye replied tartly, "Well, we haven't figured that part out yet—BUT we are going to—starting now."

"OK.," I said, "First thing—what is it we do know for sure or 'almost' for sure?"

Addy answered, "Well, we know that Mr. Callendish died in the turret attic."

"Wait!" I interrupted, "We need a notebook or something to keep track of all these ideas. Skye, have you got something to write in?"

Skye replied, "Of course—I've got a new notebook for school I haven't used."

Addy stated, "Wait—I've brought my Mom's laptop!" Addy then added dismally, "She thought I might need to work on homework."

However, grinning widely, Addy raced to her sleepover pack and pulled out the laptop. Neither Skye nor I had one—yet. Our parents seemed to live in another world.

Addy popped her laptop open, found the icon for writing, clicked on it, and immediately had the best notebook ever.

"So?" Addy continued, "What else do we know about Mr. Callendish?"

Addy—who typed fast, began to record our thoughts quickly.

Skye stated, "Well, we know that Mr. Callendish loved painting."

Ghost in the Turret

I added, "And that he created the incredible candies at the factory—that made him a success—AND a lot of money."

I could see that Addy was sifting through her ever-smart brains, so—Skye and I waited for her next comment.

"So…" Addy started thoughtfully while still in a state of concentration.

"When do you think there was a problem between Mr. Callendish and his candy factory and his love of painting? And what type of problem could it have been?"

"Well, that's not an easy question," Skye replied, raising her voice. Both Addy and I put our fingers to our lips and said quietly, "We don't want to wake your parents!"

Addy pulled her finger away from her lips. She wanted to make sure we kept our voices low and then explained, "Well, we know that Mrs. Callendish despised him painting. She just wanted him to spend all of his time at the factory making sure it was making them all the money they—or—she needed, Addy added slyly."

Skye then questioned, a bit perplexed, "When did we know that? I don't remember anything about that."

Skye looked at me for confirmation.

I said, "Well, I thought Mr. Grimly might have said something similar to that, but I can't say for sure."

Addy replied gruffly, "Well, he did! BUT let's not argue about that. I think we should go back to the Library with all the new information we have learned and do some deeper digging. But not only on his death—but EVERYTHING we can find."

"Like what?" I asked.

Addy replied, "Like all the police reports, newspaper reports, obituaries, coroner reports!"

Skye interrupted, "What is a 'coroner'?"

Addy rolled her eyes and replied, "It's the doctor who works with the police to figure out how the person died." Addy continued, "Supposedly, he committed suicide—but that was NEVER proven. We should even go to interview anyone who investigated his death or was part of the investigation."

Skye suddenly looked sickened and asked, "Addy, this seems like a lot of gruesome work—just 'to maybe,' find out who's trying to spook my house."

Addy threw up her hands, rolled her eyes, and said to Skye, "THAT is why we need to do this!"

Addy continued, "This is serious, and if we don't do something quickly to stop this "GHOST," then your parents will move!"

I quickly reinforced Addy's statement by adding, "She is so right! We—the three of us need to show your parents that it's definitely not a ghost—but only a childish prank OR a real person who wants your family OUT of the house!"

Skye gazed fearfully between Addy and me and asked, "Why would anyone want to go through such steps to make my whole family want to leave our home?"

I answered, "I don't know. But I do think that anyone who has gone through this much trouble to scare your family has a real reason, and I believe they think it might be worth killing for."

"Killing for? So then?" Addy asked intensely, "What's the next step, Leira?"

I replied, "We are back off to the library tomorrow morning. AND—we'll stay there all day and find everything that was ever documented about the Callendish's, this house, and the factory!"

Skye replied reluctantly, "As long as the two of you don't ask Liam to take us there or pick us up."

Both Addy and I started giggling for the first time in what seemed ages—at the beginning with small grins, then with broad smiles, and finally, with an outburst of laughter we couldn't contain.

Skye looked at both of us, slightly confused. Then finally replied, "Well, I thought neither of you would want to be electrocuted."

After calming myself down, I said, "I think that is the least of our worries."

I looked at Addy, who was keeping her laughter in check, and she nodded in agreement.

Skye blurted out an aggravated huff, rolled her eyes, and finally burst out, "Okay—enough for tonight! I'm tired, and… it looks like tomorrow is going to be spending another happy vacation day! So, let's go to bed, and we'll start 'The Research' tomorrow."

With that, she jumped into her bed, threw the covers up over her head, and remained silent.

Addy carefully walked over to shut the lights off and giving me one last glance to make sure I had enough blankets and that her bed was ready. Afterward, she turned off the lights, and I could hear her race to her makeshift bed next to mine very quickly.

I listened to her snuggling down and wrapping the covers tightly around her.

I whispered to her, "Hey—this isn't a tent in the desert in Arizona. We don't need to be afraid of bears, cougars, snakes, and strange ancient Indian signs like in our last adventure."

I continued quietly as I heard Addy shift in her bedding, "No one is about to die, and we don't have to rescue anyone. So let's just do some research tomorrow, and hopefully, that will be the end of it."

I felt Addy turn towards me, and I could feel her anger as she said, "Yeah—this isn't Arizona, BUT that doesn't mean that someone might not die. Besides—Rob isn't here to save us."

I responded, "No, he's not but keep him in your heart and your dreams."

I heard her rapidly turn away from me, but then listened to the soft sigh of her thinking of pleasant dreams. There was nothing more I could say tonight. I was hoping my reminder of positive thoughts and remembering the boy she had met in Arizona would help her sleep peacefully. I guess I wasn't wrong.

Tomorrow we would all research everything we could lay our hands-on and hopefully find an answer or come closer to the truth.

Skye awoke earlier than Addy and me. It was a rude awakening when she pounced on my covers and shouted, "Rise and Shine!"

Crying out in fear, I answered breathlessly but loudly, "Skye! What on earth are you doing? You scared me so badly that I can barely breathe."

Skye replied, "Well, now you know how it feels to be REALLY scared."

Addy, awakened by both Skye and me, jumped up off her inflated bed and shouted at both of us, "I've had enough! Either you two explain quickly why you're trying to frighten me to death, or I am OUT OF HERE! NOW—EXPLAIN!"

Skye, who was still planted on my 'bed' in a threatening stance—relaxed and sat down next to me. Glancing between Addy and me, she said, "Look, I'm really sorry about how I started this morning off. I know both of you are just trying to help me AND my family, and I've just let this 'THING' really get to me."

Addy and I saw tears glistening in Skye's eyes, which we knew she would never want us to see. So, we both looked downwards as she continued, while holding back the tears, "You guys are right. We just need to dig deeper about everything at the library, and I'm sure we'll come up with more clues if not an answer."

"Right then!" I answered with a typical Scottish brogue, "Let's just get some breakfast and be on our way."

Addy lightened the mood even more. She added in her musical Welsh accent, "Skye, do ya think that your mum might cook us up some Welsh rarebit tonight after our toils at the library?"

Skye and I burst out laughing, remembering when Addy first told us that her Mom was bringing Welsh 'rabbit' to our dinner party.

Skye promptly stopped laughing. After gaining her composure, she stood up next to me.

Then, she said with her natural Irish flare, "You'll be getting nothing but a wee bit of salted porridge if ya doona get on downstairs now!"

The three of us were giggling as we hurriedly got dressed and put away our bedding. Then, we headed downstairs for some breakfast.

Mrs. Finnegan was in the kitchen when we got there.

Surprised, Mrs. Finnegan asked with her thick Irish brogue, "And why are my three wee girls up so early?"

Skye grimaced, but then replied, "We're hungry."

I stepped in front of Skye to try and soften up Mrs. Finnegan.

I stated, "Mrs. Finnegan, we (Addy and I) would like to thank you for having us stay here while my parents are on vacation. We can all get our own breakfast without bothering you if you will just let us know what is easiest."

I smiled at her with sincere thanks, while Addy and Skye listened to me with perplexed confusion.

Mrs. Finnegan replied, "Well, I am off to work in 30 minutes, so I don't have time to make anything more for you, but I did fry up some bacon, and there are cereal, milk, toast, and eggs if you'd care to cook them. Or you could even make some Belgium waffles if you feel up to the challenge. I'll leave it up to the three of you."

Just as she was turning to walk away, I quickly asked, "Mrs. Finnegan? Is there any chance that your drive to work goes near or by the Library?"

She replied, "Well, yes, it does. Do you need a lift?"

Addy answered quickly, "Well, yes, we do. So, we'll have some milk, cereal, and bacon, and then we'll be ready when you are."

Mrs. Finnegan replied, "That's fine. I'll be leaving in twenty-five minutes, so don't waste any time."

We replied swiftly, "We won't."

Hurriedly, we grabbed bowls, glasses, cereal, spoons, and milk. Then we almost inhaled it to make sure we wouldn't keep Mrs. Finnegan waiting.

With the bowls and silverware rinsed off and placed in the dishwasher, we raced to the car where Mrs. Finnegan was waiting, having just started the engine.

We were off to the library and were NOT going to leave until we had all the information we needed.

Once we arrived at the library, Skye asked Addy and me, "Are we looking for the reason for his suicide—or are we looking for a murderer?"

Addy and I glanced quietly at one another, and I replied breathlessly, "We don't know."

Gathering what courage I could, I said to Skye, "Either way—we are going to solve this, and you and your family will stay here—SAFE!"

I looked at my two best friends, and we gathered hands in unison, gave a shake of confidence, and walked into the Library.

Chapter 17
The Puzzle Starts To Come Together

Addy, Skye, and I spent the whole day delving into everything we could about Mr. Callendish, his factory, his wife, and his death.

Addy took charge of every bit of information about the 'Suicide.' She left no stone unturned. She read every article written on his death, the coroner's reports, even tabloid quotes.

Skye looked into every aspect of his life at that time. She focused on the Candy factory and how it was developed. She read every article on it available and how much he loved it. But, things kept crossing paths in his interviews about his love of painting. Skye realized there was some kind of connection, but she wasn't sure what.

I concentrated my time on how they spent their time and money. Luckily, I came across a very intriguing librarian who helped me out with that part. I wasn't even a bit experienced with how to get that information. I was barely sure what I needed to know. I thought it was important to understand if Mrs. Callendish was using up her husband's money for her own pleasure.

The librarian enthusiastically helped me sift through information and gave me documented facts to confirm my suspicions.

At the end of a very long day, when we finished gathering all the information we could, we stood outside, waiting for Mrs. Finnegan to pick us up.

Addy asked excitedly, "Well, did both of you get the info you were looking for? Something that will help us put this puzzle together?"

Skye replied, "I got so much information! It was much more than I expected to get AND much more intriguing."

Addy looked at me with expectation and asked, "What about you, Leira? Did you get everything or anything to help us solve this mystery?"

I stated, "Well, I met this very interesting librarian who helped me uncover a lot of things I never would have looked for. So, yes, I got what I was looking for and A LOT more!"

Skye and Addy were almost holding their breaths for me to continue when Skye's Mom pulled up to the corner to take us home.

I gave my head a quick shake, "No," so they wouldn't talk about what we had found out at the library. We would have to wait until the three of us were alone to speak about it.

That night was the most intense, scary, and mesmerizing since our adventure started. The stories that poured back and forth were all coming together.

The first thing we had to decide was where we were going to spend the night—in the turret room or Skye's bedroom.

Skye was the first to speak out and said, "I'd rather stay in my room while we put all of this information together."

Addy agreed rather quickly, adding, "I believe we'll be thinking more clearly there than up in the Turret."

I agreed with both of them, then asked Addy to get her laptop to record our findings.

Taking a deep breath, I asked, "OK—let's start with Skye. So, what did you learn in detail about Mr. Callendish and his love of art and the candy factory?

And so, the tale started to be revealed.

Skye began, "Well, when Mr. Callendish was young, he used to buy small candies from the 5 & dime shop across the street."

Addy sniggered and replied, "The 5 & dime shop", yeah right."

Skye angered slightly, said, "Yes! When he was a young boy, there were such things as 5 and dime shops!"

I played peacemaker by telling Addy, "It's true. I've heard about them from my Grandparents and even my Dad—so hush, let Skye continue."

Skye gave me a smile of approval and continued, "Anyway, Mr. Callendish loved two things—painting and candy. He would buy at least ten candies at a time and go to his room and sketch, paint, draw or sculpt as long as the candies melted in his mouth."

"His parents always encouraged him because, for one dollar, he would stay in his room for hours, sucking on those candies and creating his artwork."

"Of course," Skye continued, "That was long before he moved here."

"This kept up until he was grown and studied Business Management in College as he knew what he wanted to do with his life. He wanted to make a Candy Factory."

Skye's story soon began to memorize Addy and me. We continued to become immersed in it as she continued.

"So." Skye continued, "Throughout his college years, he began to put together a plan of how to build his candy factory from an exceedingly small store into a big factory. He worked at a little restaurant down the street named 'The Happy Diner' and saved every penny he earned."

Skye added, "Apparently, he was such a good waiter that he earned a lot more tips than anyone else!"

"Anyway, by the time he graduated, he had everything figured out. When he needed time to put his plan together over those years, he would lock his bedroom door and work things out in his mind as he created his art!"

"Wait!" Addy interrupted. "How could he possibly create artwork when he was thinking of a candy business? It doesn't make any sense to me."

Enthusiastically, Skye said, "That is the brilliance behind his artwork! He melted the different flavors of candy in his mouth as his brain was planning how to achieve his goal. Then with the brushes and paints, he created his artwork. His hands just followed the pattern of his thoughts and the taste in his mouth!"

Skye continued, "Haven't either of you REALLY looked at his artwork? They have everything to do with taste, smell, color, organization, and achieving or building his dream."

Addy and I looked at one another in amazement. After what seemed like a long time, we both realized we hadn't paid much attention to Mr. Callendish's artwork.

Plainly, I said to Skye, "No, I never really took a good look at his work or thought to connect it with the Candy Factory."

Skye said, "Well, you both have some catching up to do then! I won't add anymore right now. Why don't you tell us what you discovered, Addy?"

Addy grimaced and stated, "Well, as you know, my task was finding out about his death (or suicide). It was kind of a gruesome experience.

Addy continued, "I was able to read all the newspaper articles about his 'supposed suicide.' I found within the three different stories that they didn't match completely. I've printed out copies, so we can go over them more thoroughly, but one of the newspapers seemed to think that it might not have been suicide! It turns out the reporter was a huge fan of Mr. Callendish's artwork and had procured many pieces of his works."

Addy continued, "So, this man spent a lot of time with him in his studio. He even commissioned Mr. Callendish to do a portrait of his wife!"

Skye questioned, "Is there anything more you found out?"

Addy replied, "Only that the coroner's report stated it was suicide—death by asphyxiation—otherwise hanging himself."

I interrupted, "I thought he died from cutting his wrist—you know—the blood…"

Addy explained, "Actually, from the reports, it looks like he might have been strangled, then someone cut his wrists. But the coroner's report was inconclusive. It seemed to me that Mrs. Callendish spoke to the police about his depression and that he had confided in her that he wished he was dead."

Addy continued, "What I don't get is that this person, Mr. Michaud, briefly said in the interview that he didn't believe Mr. Callendish killed himself. The article was short, and I think they cut off anything else he might have said. So, I think we should try and track down Mr. Michaud."

I responded, "We should definitely try and find him—as soon as possible."

Continuing, I said, "As far as my research went, I found out some interesting information. Mrs. Callendish was spending gobs of money on everything from expensive clothes and jewels to long vacations in the Caribbean!"

I added, "Her picture was in A LOT of magazines and newspaper articles. Some of the stories say how Mrs. Callendish was seen at the opening of a new fancy store and wearing one of their original creations. Or how she was attending an expensive dinner to honor someone. The list keeps going on, and I've taken notes on all of them!"

"Apparently, she left Mr. Callendish at home during her 'vacations' to run the business and work on his art."

"That was all I could find out from public records, but I think it's just the tip of the iceberg!"

I added in a mystified voice, "Remember what the letter said that we got in the mail and never showed your parents Skye?"

Skye answered, "Of course."

I reminded both Addy and Skye that the letter said something like, "I hated the Candy Factory and the candy!"

"Does that sound anything like the man we've been reading all of this documentation on? And the same man that Mr. Grimly knew?"

"If—and I say "If" because I don't know for sure and we don't have the money to hire a detective, I think Mrs. Callendish used up all of his money and then needed more."

Both Addy and Skye were fascinated by my conclusion. They both agreed that we were all on the right track. But then, Skye yawned, and Addy glanced at the clock. She stated, "It's 2 in the morning, and I think we've done enough for today. Let's get a good night's sleep and put this all together tomorrow."

I added, "A good night's sleep? So—no ghosts tonight?"

Skye replied irritably, "Not tonight, or I'll be the one scaring them away!"

Addy and I gave a tiny chuckle before we drifted off to sleep.

The following morning, we awoke about the same time, and none of us were over-tired. Apparently, our research the day before and lack of sleep for the past few nights had let us sleep soundly.

Addy woke up first, but just her yawn awakened me. Then as we both shuffled out of our beds, Skye woke up too.

Skye murmured, "So we didn't talk about what the plan is for today, because we are running out of time. My parents are putting the house up for sale this week."

Skye challenged, "How do we put together everything so quickly?"

I replied straight away, "Tonight—we stay in the Turret room!"

Chapter 18
Ready To Face The Ghost

Addy and Skye looked shocked, but I replied calmly, "There is NO Ghost or anything to harm us! We need to prove that, or it's all over."

Addy hesitated then asked, "What if you're wrong? What if there is something or someone? We didn't imagine the telephone call or the letter in the mail!"

Skye announced with determination, "We scare the ghost—or leave. All we need is the bravery to stand up to our fears."

I agreed, and Addy nodded apprehensively.

Skye asked again, "So what do we do today to prepare for this?"

I replied, "We go see Mr. Grimly and ask for some help on 'Ghost or people catching'!"

After a filling breakfast of buttermilk pancakes and mouthwatering sausage patties, we told Mrs. Finnegan that we were taking our dogs over to visit Mr. Grimly as usual. I think she was glad just to get us all out of the house!

It was about 9:30 in the morning when we arrived at his 'creepy mansion.' We never thought of it that way anymore, but we didn't want the neighborhood bullies disturbing him, so we left the rumors run rampant as they always had in the past.

Skye knocked on the door, and all three of our dogs began barking, and just as quickly, we could hear our pups' mother howling, yapping, and scratching on the inside of the door.

Mr. Grimly didn't keep us waiting long as he opened the door. He was so happy to see the three of us and Puffins' puppies.

Mr. Grimly was smiling, 'with his relatively new lips,' as he ushered us in and asked, "To what reason do I owe the pleasure of my dearest friends visit?"

Our young dogs played happily with their Mom, so we could focus on the problem we were facing.

I began, "Mr. Grimly, you know so much already about the terrible tragedy that occurred before Skye and her family moved in."

"We've spent the last few days digging through everything we could find, and we agree with you that there are NO ghosts, but—we need to prove that, before The Finnegan's put the house up for sale in a day or two."

I continued, "We know everything that was written about the suicide/ murder, and before we attempt to move ahead any further, we need your help. We'd like to go over everything we've learned in the past few days with you."

"What do you think? Can you help us? We were planning on sleeping in the Turret room tonight, so we could confront—whatever…"

Mr. Grimly leaned back in his comfortable chair and had a slight grin that made Addy, Skye, and I lean a bit forward expectantly.

Casually, he replied, "I have already given this some thought, and I think I've come up with a worthy trap."

Startled, I replied, "A trap?"

Mr. Grimly nodded yes and said, "I know there are no ghosts there, but I think our 'fake' ghosts are just up to a bit of mischief."

"I believe it's time to put a stop to their shenanigans. So, here is what I have it mind—and I'll be letting your parents know Skye—about everything, including the phone call and the letter."

Skye grimaced at that comment, but Mr. Grimly continued.

"I agree that the three of you should spend the night in 'The Turret Room' but stay dressed, alert, and pretend to go to sleep at about one o'clock in the morning."

"Skye, with your parent's permission, I will go up into the attic of the turret room about 11:00 pm. I will wait there and have someone I can trust outside, keeping an eye on the room. We will text one another if anything occurs."

Mr. Grimly asked, "How does this sound so far?"

I replied quickly, "It sounds great! I'm so glad we came to you!"

Skye asked in a mystified voice, "Who is your 'someone' you trust to help you?"

Mr. Grimly looked at each of us individually and asked, "Do you trust me?"

The three of us nodded and said out loud, "Yes! Of course."

Mr. Grimly gazed at the three of us and said, "Jeffrey!"

We were all in shock!

Addy immediately burst out, "Jeffrey? You can't be serious. He's always tormented us!"

Mr. Grimly chuckled and replied, "Yes, in the beginning. But now that he's had a chance to get to know all of you—especially you, Addy—you have to all admit that he's been quite nice."

He continued, "He's really taken a shine to you, Addy, and if I'm wrong, then tell me now because he's been keeping watch at the times when the three of you were sleeping in the Turret Room."

"Now, tell me if I'm wrong about him."

Addy, Skye, and I felt a bit ashamed hearing what Mr. Grimly had just said.

Addy spoke up first, saying, "I guess you're right. He has been genuinely nice to me since he moved in next door. I guess I've taken for granted the times he's helped me out or offered to."

Skye, who was still in a state of disbelief, added, "I can't get over that he was watching out for us. I guess it's nice, but at the same time, it's a bit creepy."

I asked Mr. Grimly directly, "Has Jeffrey seen anyone or anything while watching?"

All three of us waited anxiously for the reply.

Mr. Grimly answered thoughtfully, "One time when he was there, he saw someone leaving through the woods, and he has heard sounds coming from the Attic or The Turret room. He wasn't sure which, so he tried to stay awake to see if the attic lights came on or if someone was moving about. But after a few hours, he nodded off, and when he awoke, he knew he had to get home."

Mr. Grimly continued, "So in my opinion, if he saw someone(s) leaving through the woods, that would absolutely confirm there is no ghost. We just need to catch whoever it is red-handed!"

So, the plan was set in motion. The first uncomfortable thing the three of us had to do was meet up with Jeffrey at Mr. Grimly's place to discuss it. We had to call Jeffrey from Addy's cell phone as she was the only one who had his number.

Skye, Addy & I could not contain our laughter as Jeffrey walked up the driveway to Mr. Grimly's home. We knew Jeffrey had met with him before but had never stepped foot inside his house by himself.

Mr. Grimly gave the three of us a stern look as he had never done before because he knew if Jeffrey was to help us, then we needed to be 'nice.'

When the knock on the door sounded, Puffin began barking; Addy was the one who got up and opened the door.

I suppose she felt that he was helping us and wanted to put him at ease because of her.

Addy opened the door and, with her usual cheerful smile, said, "Come on in, Jeffrey. We were just starting to go over the plan, and I can't say how much we appreciate your helping us."

Jeffrey was in a kind of state of shock. After a long hesitation, he lifted his head up and told Addy, "Thanks." Then he proceeded very slowly up the few steps into the living room where Puffin sniffed him out thoroughly.

Looking around the living room slowly, gazing intensely at the ancient surroundings once again, he saw Mr. Grimly, Skye, and I were already sitting.

Addy spoke, "You can sit here, Jeffrey, it's a wonderful old chair and very comfortable."

As Jeffrey took a seat, Addy asked, "Would you like some lemonade?"

After clearing his throat, he replied in a bit of a shaky voice, "OK, thanks, Addy."

I think Skye and I were amused by Jeffrey's lack of courage, but we didn't say a thing because we didn't want him to back out.

Addy came back with the lemonade, set it on a coaster next to him, and then sat down next to me.

At this point, Mr. Grimly took over the conversation.

"OK!" he began. "We are here to discuss the plan to catch this prankster that has been 'haunting' your house Skye. If we don't catch him very soon, we all know that your parents may put your home up for sale."

"AND that is the last thing we want!"

Mr. Grimly continued, "So. the plan is set for tomorrow night, the three of you, Skye, Addy, and Leira, will spend the night in the Turret room. I will come up at about 11:00 pm and go into the attic. Jeffrey will hide just inside the woods at 11:00 also. Jeffrey, you should probably bring water, snacks & a good blanket. It's best if you try and catch a nap in the afternoon."

"The three of you need—motioning to Addy, Skye, and I, need to spread the word that you're sleeping in the Turret (for some reason). Josie could actually help to spread the news."

Addy chuckled at that comment because Josie (her little sister) was the neighborhood's biggest loudmouth.

Mr. Grimly continued, "Skye, I've spoken to your parents, and although they aren't thrilled at the idea, they have agreed to go along with it. They will stay up all night. Your Dad will be ready for whatever we need."

Continuing, he added reassuringly, "All of you will be safe—so there's no need to worry. There are NO GHOST's, just someone trying to scare you and possibly your family. Whoever it is, we are going to put a stop to it tomorrow night!"

"Does everyone understand? It's a regular sleepover. We don't want to scare this person or persons away. And get into bed (but stay awake) at 1:00 am—lights out, TV off. I'll be in the attic, Jeffrey will be outside, and we'll all have our phones but only use them in an emergency."

Mr. Grimly asked one more time. "Is everyone clear?"

I asked, "What happens if Jeffrey sees someone climbing up to the attic or down from the roof?"

Mr. Grimly replied, "He'll text or call me, and I'll catch him or them." Jeffrey will also have notified Mr. Finnegan, who will call the police. So be prepared if they come."

Mr. Grimly added, "If anyone has any questions pop up, then you'll have to come and see me by tomorrow."

We all got up to leave feeling slightly uneasy but knew we were in good hands.

As we were leaving, Mr. Grimly touched me on the shoulder. I turned around, and he asked, "Leira, could you stay a bit longer?"

Addy and Skye overheard but kept on walking.

I said, "Sure, what do you need?"

Mr. Grimly looked dreadfully embarrassed as he replied, "I just got one of these dang cell phones, and I have no idea how to use it."

I smiled broadly, holding back a laugh, and said, "Here, let me get you started."

It took me two and a half hours to get him to the point where he could text or call. But it was necessary. I told him I would stop by in the morning around ten and give him a refresher course. He was grateful.

"Now, we were about ready to unveil the ghost!"

Skye, Addy, and I invited Jeffrey to come home with us after I finished my training session, to discuss the plan amongst ourselves.

We decided to go to my house where there was plenty to munch on, and our living room was enormous. I didn't want Jeffrey to feel 'closed in.'

Jeffrey started the conversation by asking about the big hemlock tree that we had climbed in the woods behind my house.

Skye said strictly, "That's only part of the initiation into our secret club!"

Addy and I glanced at one another quickly because we had no idea what she was talking about.

Skye glanced at us and gave her head a tiny shake. 'No.' I guess she would tell us later.

Addy asked Jeffrey, "Do you have everything you need to bring at home, or is there anything we can help you with?"

Jeffrey brightened up as Addy questioned him. Then after thinking a moment, he replied, "Well, I really could use a good flashlight, and what if one of 'THEM' comes after me? What should I do? Do you have any ideas?"

I quickly replied, "Well, my Dad has a 'fondness' for flashlights, so I can definitely get you two great ones." Thinking for a moment, I added, as far as confronting any 'bad guys,' I have four pepper spray canisters. They're small and can easily fit into your coat. Just make sure you can get at them quickly."

Everyone was impressed with my solutions. I smiled happily and went to get the items.

When I arrived back in the living room, Addy was waiting with a chain she always wore around her neck.

She said to me, "Leira, let me have the canisters of pepper spray, and I'll attach them to this necklace. Then, Jeffrey can wear it around his neck, and he can use them easily without worrying where they are."

As I handed the pepper spray cans over to Addy, I whispered to her, "But isn't that the necklace that your grandmother gave you?"

Addy whispered back, "Yes—but don't say a word."

I nodded while Addy finished stringing on the canisters, then turned and placed the long necklace over Jeffrey's head.

He blushed.

Addy said, "Keep the necklace safe, or you might lose the pepper spray!"

I announced, "OK everyone, I think we all need to go home, have a large dinner to eat, and meet up at Skye's house tomorrow at nine or ten o'clock. We may come up with some questions before we go to sleep tonight."

I continued, "Jeffrey, you have your instructions, so make sure you sleep, eat, and pack what you need. It's supposed to be a bit chilly tomorrow night, so don't forget your coat."

Skye added, "And whatever you do, make sure you get a good night's sleep!"

Jeffrey snorted, then got up and walked out of Leira's house to pack. He turned just as he was about to close the door and gave Addy one more glance and a small smile.

Chapter 19

Not For Sale— You Can't Threaten Us

I said, "Well, Ladies, let's hope by tomorrow night, we'll be prepared to catch whoever is behind this, and Skye won't be moving anywhere."

With that said, the three of us traipsed back to Skye's house to try and eat then get to sleep. I thought to myself, 'I don't think I'll be able to take a bite or get much sleep tonight.'

As I smelled the aroma, I knew Mrs. Finnegan had made Macaroni and cheese (my favorite). A yummy salad was next to my plate with her homemade Russian dressing (Mayonnaise mixed with ketchup), which I loved.

But there was one more dish Mr. Finnegan was bringing over from the stove, and as he placed it on the hot pad, I cried out, "NO! Not Brussel sprouts!"

"Please, Mrs. Finnegan, I really choke if I try to eat them."

Mr. Finnegan smiled as always and said, "They're just little cabbages, and they're good for you."

Skye's Mom said encouragingly, "You only have to eat two, and if you don't like them, I'll just give you extra salad."

Slightly relieved, I said, "OK."

With disgust, I looked down at my plate and ate my salad with half of my mac & cheese, then tried to eat one Brussel sprout; I held my nose and chewed on one for quite a while as I didn't think I could swallow it. Finally, I did, but I gagged as it was going down. I hurried to take a couple bites of my mac & cheese and drank a lot of blueberry flavored seltzer before looking back at my plate. I started to gag at the thought of eating another one.

Skye's Mom took pity on me and said, "Alright, I think you've proven just how bad these are to you. I had the same reaction to asparagus. So, for tonight I'll just give you some extra salad. Next time I'll know and make green beans or broccoli instead." I was so thankful that I got up and gave her a big hug and asked, "Is it OK if I go up and unpack now?"

She nodded but added, "You need to finish your salad first."

I did, and then raced up the stairs. Of course, I had everything already unpacked. It was 7:30, but I thought it better to be early than late, so I headed back downstairs.

Mr. Finnegan reminded me, "Don't forget to take Fluffums outside for a short walk, and she'll need her dinner too."

I moaned and proceeded over to my house with Skye, to fill up her dog food bowl, sprinkle some cheese on it and give her a fresh bowl of water.

I looked at Skye and pleaded, "Could you please come with me to take her for a short walk?"

Skye said, "Yeah, just let me go get Shugar, and we'll walk them together."

Skye was back in a little over a minute, and we walked the two pups while they did their 'business,' then I returned Fluffums home.

Skye opened her front door, and to our complete surprise, Addy answered the door!

Surprised, Skye asked her, "Why are you here so early?"

Addy replied, "It's already ten minutes before eight, so I wouldn't call it that early. And besides, you're here too."

We watched a little TV and decided not to speak about what was planned for tomorrow. We finally laid down, threw soft blankets over ourselves, closed our droopy eyes, and fell sound asleep.

Mrs. Finnegan woke us up the following morning, along with Shugar, who leaped onto my bed and wouldn't stop licking and nuzzling me.

Mrs. Finnigan strangled a burst of laughter and, after catching her breath, said, "Breakfast is starting to get cold if you three don't hurry up."

Panicking, I asked, "What time is it?"

She rolled her eyes and said, "It's 7:30, so you'll have plenty of time to eat, unpack and get up to the Turret room for your sleepover. And Leira, don't forget that you have to see Mr. Grimly this morning and that Jeffrey is coming over at 10:00 AM to go over everything. Now get yourselves out of bed and have breakfast before it's cold."

We untangled ourselves from the bedding, and Shugar raced downstairs with Skye, Addy, and me as we plunked down into the soft dining room chairs.

I finished my breakfast quickly and then ran down the street to Mr. Grimly's Manor.

He opened the door just as I was about to knock on it.

He said, "I was watching for you to come. I spent half the night trying to make sure I knew how to use this thing. I'll tell you right now that technology and I don't like each other much."

I smiled warmly and said, "That's OK. I don't like a lot of it either. But, Addy is a wiz at this, so she helps Skye, and I learn new things a bit at a time."

We spent almost an hour going over how to text and call. But I could tell Mr. Grimly had it down just fine. I think he needed just a little boost of confidence.

At ten o'clock, I abruptly stated, "I'm sorry, Mr. Grimly, but I need to get back to Skye's as Jeffrey is coming over to review everything with us."

Mr. Grimly replied, "That's OK. I will see all of you at about eleven o'clock. Until then, try and stay calm."

I gave him a hug and replied, "OK, I'll do my best!"

On my walk back to Skye's, I muttered to myself, "Yeah, right—keep calm."

Jeffrey was already there when I arrived, so the four of us passed out a list of what each of us had to do.

We went over the list very carefully to make sure everyone was clear about what we had to do. At noon, Mrs. Finnegan brought us some tuna fish sandwiches, chips, and sparkling water for lunch.

Jeffery left at one o'clock, and all of us were supposed to take a nap from two to three.

Skye said, "I'm not really tired. Do you want to take the pups for a run around the block to tire us out a bit?"

Addy replied, "I think that's a super idea. Let's go."

We let the Finnegans know and set out to gather the dogs.

Panting, while only halfway around the block, I said to Skye and Addy, "I think we need to spend more time in the desert and climbing trees."

Skye breathlessly replied, "Agreed."

When we finally got back and put the pups away, I said, "OK—nap time.

It was precisely two o'clock when we laid down. Skye said, "I think I'll take a shower first."

Addy said, "If I'm not asleep by the time you finish—I'll take one too."

I sniffed under my arm and added, "I definitely need a shower also."

All three of us ended up taking a shower and drying our hair. It was after three o'clock before we crawled into bed to nap. Addy fell asleep pronto as usual.

Skye said, "How does she do that? Every time she lays down, within three minutes, she's sound asleep, and not even a woodpecker could wake her up." We both giggled, then tried our best to take a nap.

Addy woke us up at 4:30, and she was wide awake. Skye and I were a might befuddled. We rubbed our eyes, yawned, and sat up.

We shuffled downstairs to check in with the Finnegans.

Mrs. Finnegan came out of the living room and asked us, "Is there anything you girls need? You know Mr. Finnegan, and I will be up all night, and all you need to do is call us on your cell or use the intercom system we had installed."

"There's plenty to eat and drink upstairs, and I've made sure Liam is away to his friends' tonight, so you don't need to worry about him. Are you all OK?"

We each nodded yes, and I said, "Thank you, Mrs. Finnegan. All three of us want this straightened out so you won't move."

She responded, "I know, and I hope in the morning, everything will come out fine. Now get upstairs and let's catch these 'People/Ghosts'!"

I agreed with her.

Addy stated, "Come on up to the Turret room. I've got pizza ready to microwave and spooky movies to watch. Just what we need, right?"

Skye and I glanced at each other a bit perplexed, but Skye said, "Yeah, I guess so, let's go."

Addy and I raced up the two flights of stairs to the turret. We spent the next few hours re-watching a scary dinosaur movie, then a funny one that we had seen several times. We ate our pizza and polished off all of the popcorn. It was really awesome. It was almost 12:30 AM, and Mr. Grimly hadn't shown up yet.

I said after a big yawn, "I'm getting sleepy. How about something to perk us up?"

Addy said, "Good idea. Is it alright if I get an energy drink to make sure we don't fall asleep?"

Skye replied, "Of course. Could you get one for me too? How about you, Leira? Do you want one?"

I asked, "Do you have any of those strawberry ones that I like so much?"

Skye said, "Yep. So, Addy, get one strawberry for Leira, one grape for me, and one of whatever you want."

Addy quickly got out of bed, went to the little fridge, got the three drinks, and then handed them to us.

I asked her, "What flavor did you choose?"

She replied cheerfully, "Cherry, of course."

We gulped our small bottles down and every now and then whispered about what was happening or how the school would be when we went back.

When we were supposed to go to bed, Skye shut off both the TV and the lights, then we crawled into bed with our clothes on.

I softly asked, "Are both of you wide awake?"

Skye and Addy quickly answered, "Yes." Skye continued, "But let's whisper until something happens or it's morning."

We paused quite often to listen for any sounds.

Mr. Grimly had come up at 12:45 am and climbed into the attic. None of us were brave enough to accompany him. We made sure he had enough to eat and drink, and Skye's Dad had put a soft chair that could be raised up to relax his feet. He included some warm blankets so his old bones wouldn't get too chilly.

Shortly after 2:00 AM, I thought I heard something outside. I whispered, "Did either of you hear that?"

Addy replied, "I heard something. Do you think it was Jeffrey?"

Skye groggily added, "I'm not sure, but I think I might have drifted off for a moment."

Addy whispered, "Ergh! Get yourself another energy drink."

Skye got up to get one, and we heard something louder from outside!

The entrance to the Turret Attic was above my head, and I poked it open a little way, and asked very quietly, "Mr. Grimly—are you awake? Did you hear those noises?"

Mr. Grimly said quietly, "Yes, now, the three of you get over near the door. I've beeped your parents Skye and Jeffrey too."

"If you hear my whistle blow, then go directly to The Finnegan's room."

I quickly closed the attic door, then Addy, Skye, and myself huddled next to the open doorway downstairs.

I carried an old but strong baton I used in the past. Skye held her brother's baseball bat, and Addy brought a tire iron she had 'borrowed' from her Dad's car.

We were ready!

Until that moment, we were calm but scared at the same time. It all seemed unreal now that it was happening, but suddenly things changed.

We heard breaking glass in the attic. We listened to the cries of more than one person and the banging of the piano. During all of this, Mr. Finnegan came racing through the door and hustled up into the attic.

Within moments, things seemed to quiet down a bit, although we could hear angry words being spoken.

Jeffrey was the first one to descend from the attic. He looked utterly bedraggled and was trying to put on a good face. Mrs. Finnegan hurriedly came in with towels and wrapped one around Jeffrey.

Ghost in the Turret

I tried to question him as she ushered him out the door, but it didn't feel right. Addy and I just glanced awkwardly at each other.

Next to emerge was Mr. Grimly. He had a small cut on his temple's right side but kept the blood under control with his handkerchief.

We waited for the next person to come down, and it was Liam's nasty friend Frankie.

Mr. Grimly told him, "The police have already been called and will be here shortly! So, don't give anyone here a hard time." Mr. Grimly tied Frankie's hands quickly behind his back.

We could hear the sirens coming in the background.

Lastly, Skye's brother Liam came down through the attic passage with his father holding him by the scruff of the neck.

Mr. Finnegan was furious. He couldn't believe his own son was a part of this, never mind that he may have been the one to come up with the plan.

Why would he have done it? Why would he want to move? Why would he want to scare three young girls this way?

I guess they were questions that would have to be answered later.

The police arrived and took Frankie and Liam into custody for breaking and entering—to begin with. They said it would get sorted out the next day with Mr. Finnegan and Frankie's Dad.

Mrs. Finnegan had walked Jeffrey home where his Mom had gotten him thoroughly dried off and put him to bed after a yummy bowl of hot chicken noodle soup.

After she arrived home, Mrs. Finnegan told us what happened before having us all put on our jammies and climbing into bed.

Before she closed the door, she said, "See, I told you—NO GHOSTS."

The three of us were too exhausted and fell sound asleep within minutes.

The following morning, we ate breakfast, dressed in a hurry, and 'casually' asked Mrs. Finnegan if it was safe now to go into the attic.

She responded, "I don't see why not, although I wouldn't jump up and down. But don't forget to take care of your pet's first!"

111

We felt stupid that we had forgotten them and raced to take care of them.

Afterward, as we walked back to Skye's, I said, "One big part of the mystery is solved—now we have to figure out the rest."

Skye replied, "Yeah, the most dangerous part."

Chapter 20
5 Heads Crack The Case

We hurried back to Skye's afterward and climbed up into the Turret room.

Addy said shakily, "I kind of wish Jeffrey was here."

Skye sniggered and replied, "I'll tell him you said that—I'm sure it will make him happy."

"SKYE Finnegan! Don't you dare or I'll never speak to you again."

I pushed myself in between the two of them, and sternly said, "Remember why we are going up there?"

I gave an intense stare towards the opening of the attic. "Are we ready to do what we set out to do?"

"We need to find proof that he didn't kill himself. Ready?"

Hesitantly we climbed the stairs that we pulled down from the attic opening. We had been so afraid of the attic and ghosts for so long that it took a bit more nerve than we figured.

Skye went first but waited just to the side of the door opening. I followed next and stood beside Skye as Addy made her way up.

When the three of us were all there, we held our flashlights to survey the places closest to us.

Luckily, it was almost dawn, and there was a dim light coming through the attic windows from the rising sun.

After shining our lights across the whole space of the small attic, we set out in different directions to look more closely at each spot.

Addy muffled a scream and stammered, "Look!"

Skye and I hurried over and looked closely at what Addy was shining her light on.

"It's blood!" Skye stated. "This must be where he died."

I said, slightly relieved, "We already saw that when the Finnegans brought us up here last week."

Addy looked completely embarrassed.

The blood was soaked into the floorboards awfully close to where his painting easel was.

I thought a few minutes and said, "If he killed himself here with a knife, then why is the easel still here but none of his other supplies? Don't you think that's odd?"

Addy replied, "Not if his wife had everything thrown away."

"OK," said Skye, "Then why didn't she get rid of the easel along with his other stuff? Why didn't she have the floorboards replaced? She was selling the house so no one would want those reminders."

Addy stifled a laugh and said, "Well, your parents didn't mind!"

Skye shot a scathing look towards Addy, and Addy immediately removed the grin from her face.

After another few minutes of thinking about what we'd seen, the sun was almost up. I looked down at the dried blood again and noticed a brighter red splash just a foot or two away from the large spot.

Suddenly, ideas were forming in my mind, and I blurted out, "We need to go get Mr. Grimly and bring him here, pronto!"

Skye and Addy asked in unison, "What?"

I replied, "Never mind. You two stay here, and I'll go get him."

Both Addy and Skye were totally perplexed and just watched me scramble down the stairs and out of the room.

Skye asked Addy, "Do you think we should follow her or get one of my parents?"

Addy opened her eyes wide and replied, "I don't think so. She's on to something, and I would feel better if Mr. Grimly was here to listen to her."

As it turned out, they only had to wait a few minutes before Mr. Grimly and I arrived.

Surprised, Skye asked, "How did you get here so fast?

I said, "Mr. Grimly noticed some clues that I didn't see. So, he was on the way back to check it out. I explained a bit about my thoughts on the few minutes we had together."

Mr. Grimly said, "Leira, you go first."

Blushing, I said, "I noticed this splash of blood that wasn't near the large spot where he 'cut his wrists.' Upon looking at it more closely, I realized it wasn't blood after all! That—pointing at the spot, must be paint. That really intrigued me because there is no other color of paint on the floor anywhere else in the room."

I asked, "Mr. Grimly, could you continue, please?"

"Well.", Mr. Grimly said, "I noticed while sitting up here waiting, that the big heater-air-conditioning unit that was up here had been boarded off."

"Mr. Callendish always worked in comfort, so therefore Rupert had the need of the unit. I thought it was odd that it had been boarded up. So, I think we should call the police and have them here to take away that part of the wall-with your parent's permission, of course."

As Mr. Grimly called the police and Skye woke her parents, the three of us waited in the attic, wondering if we were going to be fools or heroes.

Mr. and Mrs. Finnegan were with us when the police arrived (again), and Mr. Grimly walked them through our ideas.

The police got Mr. and Mrs. Finnegans permission to open the boarded part of the wall (carefully), and unbelievably we found one of Mr. Callendish's paintings. It was incredibly beautiful. The piece of artwork showed an elderly but vital man with a walking stick moving forward through some sheep on a hillside with Ben Nevis in Scotland behind him. He was smiling with warmth and happiness.

I knew about Ben Nevis (the highest mountain in Scotland) because my Mom told me many stories and showed me tons of pictures and movies that she—and Aunt Debbie had made.

Skye asked, "Why would anyone board this up? It's an incredible piece."

I replied after looking at it more closely, "See there?" I pointed to the slight red 'lines' across both wrists. I continued, "It could be thought of as a deep wrinkle, but I don't think so."

The police were patiently listening, but with interest and suspicion.

They looked intently at the red paint spot I had pointed out to them and then back at the red color in the crease. They seemed to match.

The Chief said, "Given's, take this down to our lab team and see if the paint is the same."

Policeman Givens was an avid artist and fan of Mr. Callendish's work. He even owned two pieces.

Officer Given's asked, "Chief, I'd like to remove the backing of the painting if you don't mind?"

Chief Myrtle asked, "What on earth for?"

Given's replied, "I own two of the deceased paintings, and he told me both times that he sometimes puts his signature or note attached to the back."

"I'm wondering if he left something behind this one."

Addy, Skye, The Finnegan's, and I were listening in amazement. This was a lot to take in on little or no sleep, but we were mesmerized."

Chief Myrtle replied, "Sounds like it should be done, but we don't want to damage the value, so be cautious."

"Yes, sir!" he replied. "I know what I'm doing."

Carefully he gently removed the paper backing, and there inside was a note!

Everyone (I think) let out a gasp of surprise.

Addy hurriedly said, "Quick! Read it!"

Officer Givens got a nod of approval from his Chief before starting to read.

After clearing his throat, he began,

"To whomever may read this, I must be brief as I only have a few months left (cancer). My wife doesn't know, but she wants me dead anyway, as her first husband died mysteriously."

"I leave behind my favorite painting as I've always loved Scotland, and I'm there in spirit now."

"I don't know how she'll do it, but I'll try and leave a clue. I believe her first husband was poisoned by techolic acid, which absorbs quickly. And because she had him cremated the following day, there was no way to prove it."

"She hates my painting and just wants me working 14 hours a day at the candy factory. Well, that's what my Da left me, so I tried to do right by him and leave it to my children, but alas, there were none. My wife will receive nothing upon my death, so she'll be off scouting for a 'new' catch. I hope she never finds one or that the police catch her first."

This is an addendum to my will. "Whoever may find this painting (excluding my wife), if you bring her to justice, the painting is yours to do with as you will. Keep it, sell it, whatever makes the best sense to you."

Kind Regards,

Mr. Rupert Callendish"

The entire attic was suddenly completely quiet. I think we were all in shock.

Officer Given's finally cleared his throat and said to all of us, "I think we have enough evidence here to prove or disprove his statement. Apparently, he painted those small lines in red paint after his wife slit his wrists and falling to the ground with the paintbrush in his hand made the small splash of red paint that you figured out Leira."

Officer Givens resumed, "I believe in tidying things up; she stashed the painting where you've found it, without noticing the two little 'additions' to the painting. It would have taken a long time to bleed out through the wrists. So, he must have had enough time and energy left to paint the tiny clues."

"Chief Myrtle, what do you think?"

Chief Myrtle answered, "I agree, but at this point, it's circumstantial evidence. So, we'll need a bit of time to investigate Mrs. Callendish, the paint, and the note along with his financial records and will."

We'll be in touch with you as soon as we have any news. You can trust us when I say, "I'm very proud of all of you for 'catching your Ghosts' last night. And, for leading us to evidence that might put a murderer in prison. Most importantly, you would be absolving a man who was thought to have committed suicide."

The following day, Addy, Skye, Mr. Grimly, and I sat on his front porch. Our parents and we had been helping to fix up, so it was far sturdier than previously. I had called Jeffrey as we wanted to share with everything that had happened.

After he arrived and took a spot near Addy, I stated happily, "Well, it didn't take very long for our Police to wrap things up. They were quick to match the paint and redo the autopsy to confirm he was poisoned just before she cut his wrists. And we all read this morning that Mrs. Callendish was arrested before she could marry that nice old man with all his money.

Skye added, "And don't forget that the police also traced the letter and the phone call back to her.

"Right!" I said.

How long has it been? Eleven days?"

Addy replied, well twelve, if you counted the night when they arrested Liam and Frankie."

Skye smiled and added, "I'm just so grateful I don't have to move! You guys are stuck with me for a while."

Mr. Grimly replied, "You know life has been a lot nicer this last year, so how about a group hug?"

As we stood up so the four of us could hug, Jeffrey stood up with an excellent camera and said, "I've got to get this picture!"

Jeffrey got his picture, and then Skye suggested, "Jeffrey, I'm good with cameras, so why don't I get a picture of the four of you, with you and Addy in the center."

Jeffery blushed as he handed Skye the camera, and she stood back to take our picture, but I knew what she had in mind (and so did Mr. Grimly).

So just before Skye took the picture, Mr. Grimly and I each took a step to the side so Skye could get an excellent image of Addy and Jeffrey.

It was tough for me not to laugh as I said, "There might be a wee bit of bickering when the photo's come out."

www.ingramcontent.com/pod-product-compliance
Lightning Source LLC
Jackson TN
JSHW021906121224
75335JS00003B/17